Friend or Foe 2

Mimi

Lock Down Publications and Ca$h
Presents
Friend or Foe 2
A Novel by *Mimi*

Mimi

Lock Down Publications
P.O. Box 944
Stockbridge, Ga 30281

Visit our website @
www.lockdownpublications.com

Copyright 2020 by Mimi
Friend or Foe 2

First Edition November 2020
Printed in the United States of America

This is a work of fiction. Names, characters, places, and incidents either are products of the author's imagination or are used fictitiously. Any similarity to actual events or locales or persons, living or dead, is entirely coincidental.

Lock Down Publications
Like our page on Facebook: Lock Down Publications @
www.facebook.com/lockdownpublications.ldp
Cover design and layout by: **Dynasty Cover Me**
Book interior design by: **Shawn Walker**
Edited by: **Mia Rucker**

Stay Connected with Us!

Text **LOCKDOWN** to 22828 to stay up-to-date with
new releases, sneak peaks, contests and more…
Thank you.

Submission Guideline

Submit the first three chapters of your completed manuscript to ldpsubmissions@gmail.com, subject line: Your book's title. The manuscript must be in a .doc file and sent as an attachment. Document should be in Times New Roman, double spaced and in size 12 font. Also, provide your synopsis and full contact information. If sending multiple submissions, they must each be in a separate email.

Have a story but no way to send it electronically? You can still submit to LDP/Ca$h Presents. Send in the first three chapters, written or typed, of your completed manuscript to:

LDP: Submissions Dept
Po Box 944
Stockbridge, Ga 30281

DO NOT send original manuscript. Must be a duplicate.

Provide your synopsis and a cover letter containing your full contact information.

Thanks for considering LDP and Ca$h Presents.

**Previously in
Friend or Foe: Unforgivable Sins**

Mimi

Feeling Thy Self

It was now March, and it had been two months since Sasha had spoken to, seen, or heard from her best friends. She expected Amekia not to talk to her but was surprised when she didn't get an answer from Carmen and Jade. She called them for two weeks straight before she finally gave up and tried to get her head back into her marriage. Balancing work, home, and a side piece was starting to become a bit much for her.

The relationship between her and Nas was kept under wraps, due to Sasha being his attorney. She was putting her job at risk by seeing him. Sasha tried her darndest to stay away from Nas, but after the first night they spent together, she was hooked. It was like she was a crackhead and he was the crack. He bought her gifts, ate her pussy and ass, and took time to listen to her. These were all things that Brandon didn't do, which made it easier for Sasha to fall for Nas.

The gifts that she received from Nas were ones that she only saw celebrities wear. Her wardrobe grew extensively, causing Brandon to become a little suspicious. She would lie and say that she found the items at Goodwill. Every time she went to see Nas, she would feel guilty and vow that she would end things before she got too deep. She thought that she had a handle on things, but truth be told, she'd lost all control of the situation the first night she slept with him. Sasha didn't know that when the time was right, Nas was going to do everything in his power to make Sasha his.

Brandon felt that his marriage was on the brink of ending because there was something that changed in his wife that he couldn't pinpoint. He suspected that she had been cheating, but the only thing that he found when he went snooping was texts from her clients, and nothing more. He was worried for his girls. Sasha had picked up more hours at work and barely had time to spend with them as a family. Now he knew what she was feeling when he would be out late.

"Sasha can you come in here so we can talk?" Brandon called from the kitchen. Sasha was in the living room, watching a T.V show with the girls for the first time in weeks. He knew that she was going to be leaving for the night. It was Saturday, and from what he knew, girls' night was still going on. It was just that now Sasha no longer hosted the antics at their house when it was her turn. She told him that she wanted to be able to give him and the girls privacy for them to do whatever they wanted without her and her girls being in the way.

"Talk about what, Brandon? I'm trying to spend some time with the girls before I head out for girls night," she responded as she walked into the kitchen.

Brandon looked at her from head to toe. She was dressed in black distressed jeans with a gold silk blouse and black Red Bottom heels. His eyebrows raised at the sight of the new expensive shoes.

"Where did you get the shoes from?" He asked.

"Is that what you wanted to talk about? I told you I found them at a Goodwill last week. That's how I know you haven't been listening to anything that I say."

"Did you tell me?" He tried to remember the conversations that they had last week, and he honestly couldn't remember having any conversation about her new pair of shoes.

"Yes, I did."

"I don't remember. And no, that is not why I wanted to talk to you. Is there something that you need to tell me?"

A look of fear crossed Sasha's face but left just as quickly as it had come. She said, "No."

"Are you sure? Because it seems like you're spending more time away from home."

"Yeah, to make more money."

"And it seems like your attitude has changed. You're more arrogant than I remember you being."

Sasha sighed. This was not what she wanted to have a conversation about before she went to go see Nas. Whenever she would get into it with Brandon, it seemed like her attitude would carry over to her visit with Nas. To her, it wasn't the right thing to do because Nas had done nothing wrong to her.

"I'm thriving in my career and finally making as much as the men do at my job. I may be feeling myself a little bit, but that doesn't equate to me being arrogant."

"I beg to differ. Anyhow, I believe that there is something serious going on. Maybe you are having a mid-life crisis or something. I just would like it if you started to make time for the family. If not for me, then for them girls. They ask every night why you aren't home, and to tell them you are working is making them feel like you'd rather put work first."

Sasha rolled her eyes, placed one hand on her hip, and the other on the island that separated them. She spoke maliciously, "If that was the case, they are both old enough to express that to me themselves. So why haven't they? Is it them, or is it you?"

"Dammit, Sasha, stop being so fucking defensive. You got on my ass about being at work all of the time. I've stopped working so much. Now you are doing the same thing, and I'm asking you to cut back on some of the hours."

"And if I don't? What you gonna do? Leave? Nah, you won't do that. And you know why you won't do that?"

"Why won't I? You don't have time for us no more, Sasha. How much begging do I have to do in order for you to keep your ass home?"

"You ain't got to beg and do shit. You won't leave because you know that I know that you were cheating. You were just so crafty with hiding it, that I never found any proof. That's the difference between us. While you were sticking your dick in whatever bitch you was cheating with, I was at home, cooking, cleaning, taking care of the girls, and working. Now it's your turn to experience how I felt. I'm not out here giving away pussy, I'm working," Sasha stated. She was done with the conversation and she turned to walk away from her husband. She hated to lie, but she had to do what she had to do.

She grabbed her jacket from the door. Ignoring Brandon calling her name, she walked out of the door and to her car. She was fuming. He had a lot of nerve. She reached into her purse and grabbed her cell phone as she put her car in reverse, and began to dial Jade's phone number. When she had gotten the voicemail, she remember that they all turned their backs on her and weren't speaking with her. She threw her phone into the passenger seat and screamed in frustration. The only person that she had to talk to was Nas. Finding comfort in that, she put the petal to the metal and made her way to his house. She knew he was gonna have a meal cooked, some good wine, a listening ear, and some amazing dick to sling her way.

Time flew by when Sasha got to Nas' house. To Sasha, there was never enough time in the day to spend time with Nasir. When she arrived, she decided that she would leave her home problems at the door and focus on him. It was she who catered to him. She cooked dinner, she ran him a bath, she massaged his body, and she fucked him while making his toes curl.

It was almost two in the morning when Sasha's thoughts began to get the best of her. Guilt set in, as usual, and she was ready to run home. This time, she replayed the conversation she had with her husband before she left, and decided to stay.

"What's on your mind, sweetheart?" Nas asked. They were laying on their backs and Sasha's head was resting in the crook of his arm. She thought that he had fallen asleep and jumped when he began to speak.

"Just the usual shit," she admitted.

Nas turned onto his side to face Sasha and said, "Why do you do that to yourself?"

"Do what?"

"Make yourself feel guilty. You said so yourself that your husband was cheating."

"I don't have any proof that he was, Nasir. I was just accusing him because of his actions and the way he began to move. For all I know, he could have actually been working."

Nas laid back down and dropped the subject. He knew some things that Sasha didn't know but he didn't want to put it out in the open unless she was willing to be with him. Her husband wasn't what he was portraying to be, and he had all the proof that Sasha needed in order to leave him. He had to play his cards right. He stroked her face with his available hand and rolled over to face her again. He placed a kiss on her lips and sat up. He turned the lamp on and looked at Sasha.

"You know that I love you, right? You know that I'm willing to do anything to make you mine, right?" Nas rambled.

Sasha sighed as she sat up on the edge of the bed. She was tired of this same line of questions when she would come over. With the guilt that was weighing on her heart, she couldn't deal with his shit right at the moment.

"Yes, I know all of those things, Nasir, but right now I can't focus on that."

"What if I told you that I had proof of your husband cheating?"

Sasha's throat became dry. She paused in her movements. She listened to her heartbeat in her ears as she tried to comprehend what she'd heard. In a shaky voice she asked, "What?"

He climbed from out of the bed and walked over to his closet. She watched as he pushed a panel in and slid it out of the way, giving him access to a safe. After he punched in the code, he pulled a brown envelope from the safe and made his way back to the bed.

"In this envelope is all the proof that you need. Although you didn't need it because you are a woman, and when women feel it in their gut that their man is cheating, nine times out of ten, you are right. I told you from the very beginning that, when I want something, I go through whatever hoops I need to in order to get it. I did just that to make sure that I got you. I love you, Sasha, and I want you to divorce Brandon and move in with me with the girls. We don't have to get married right away, but we can work on that. You deserve so much more than what that joker is providing for you. If I give you this information, would you consider doing just that?"

Sasha sat there flabbergasted. The exact information that she had been searching for was right in her face. But what Nasir wanted her to do, would it be worth it? Would the evidence be damage enough for her to file for a divorce from her husband and be with Nas full time? Sasha sat on the bed conflicted by what was going on. She questioned if she even wanted to see what was in the envelope.

Nasir placed the envelope on the bed and walked out of the room. No doubt he was testing to see if she would look in it while he was gone. The envelope was burning a hole in her and she needed to know. Picking up the envelope, she cautiously opened it up and pulled out everything that was in there. The contents was mostly pictures and her mouth dropped at every last one of them. She couldn't believe what she was seeing. When she came to the end of the pile, there was evidence of text messages upon text messages between her husband and his mistress. At that moment, she decided that she would consider being with Nasir. Yes, she was doing what Brandon had done. But in her mind, Brandon had done the deed first, and she was getting her revenge.

Sasha placed the papers back inside of the envelope and placed it inside of her purse for when she needed it to confront Brandon. Her heart was beyond broken. Nasir still hadn't made it back inside of the room, so she made her way into the bathroom and cried her eyes out. Little did she know, Nasir was watching the whole time, and a smile formed on his face as he watched his plan unfolding. He was sure that it would be a matter of time before she would be in his house.

Mimi

April Showers Bring May Flowers... And a Baby

Amekia was finally nearing her ninth month, and her belly poked out as if she was carrying a basketball. After her fight with Sasha, she took a leave of absence at work and decided to do everything she could to minimize her stress levels. She cut her friends off, and stayed home, only leaving to get food. She had done everything under the sun to keep her mind busy. She would read, watch TV, and even taught herself to crochet.

In the short amount of time, she had completed several outfits for her daughter. Since she didn't have a baby shower, she ordered everything that she would need for her daughter through Amazon and Walmart. Having peace of mind was the best feeling in the world, but there was something missing in her life that she couldn't help but to notice, and that was her girls.

This was the longest that she hadn't talked to them. And while she was trying to make sure that she was stress free, they still ran through her mind. She even thought about Sasha. Amekia had just let the delivery people out, after they had put together her daughters crib, and she sat on the couch. Picking up her phone, she tried Jade first, but didn't get an answer. Next was Carmen.

"It's about fucking time you called one of us," Camren yelled into the phone.

Tears brimmed under Amekia's eyes and she instantly felt bad. She mumbled into the phone, "I'm sorry."

"Oh no, don't cry, Amekia. I was only playing," Carmen responded, while kicking herself for saying something.

"No, you're right. I should have called one of y'all sooner, instead of shutting y'all out. I know that you and Jade have been trying to contact me, but that argument with Sasha just did it for me."

"Fuck that hussy, and the horse she rode on. She hasn't tried to contact anyone since that day."

"I figured that she wouldn't have contacted me, but you and Jade haven't spoken to her?"

"Nope. We chewed her ass out when you left, so of course, she wouldn't reach out to us. I don't know what's up with Jade either. I've been trying to call her for weeks now and she won't answer. Her car isn't in her driveway and the school said that she took a leave of absence for medical reasons."

Amekia gasped and asked, "Medical reasons? What for? What's wrong with her?"

"I'm not sure. The last time I saw her, she was fine. I spoke to her a few days before she just disappeared, and she was telling me that I needed to help her to break into your house to make sure that you were okay."

Amekia chuckled and then got serious. She asked, "If no one has heard from her, then how does anyone know that she is okay? This is why y'all should have listened years ago when I said we should have each other's house keys in case of an emergency."

"Damn, you sure did say that years ago."

"How does anyone know she's okay? If she left work for medical reasons, how do we know if she's not laying in her house dead? Did anybody think to send the police to her house to do a wellness check?"

"How do you think I know that she's not dead? I did that already, and they contacted me and let me know that she was fine. She smelled of alcohol, but she was fine. Our friend is going through something, and just like you did, I'm sure that she will reach out when she gets ready to."

Amekia couldn't stop herself from crying. In just a short amount of time, their group had broken up quicker than a 90's R&B group. Carmen tried to console her but hearing her friend cry brought tears to her own eyes. Nothing needed to be said. They both cried for what used to be a sisterhood and wondered if they would ever be able to recover from this.

"Owww," Amekia moaned out. A sharp pain starting in her back and moving its way to her pelvis caused her tears to stop.

"What happened? Are you okay?" Carmen asked, drying her own tears.

"No, I don't think so. I just had a sharp pain in my back, and then it moved to my pelvis. I think it may be contractions."

"Oh my God. Denise. Denise. Amekia thinks that she's having contractions," Carmen yelled.

Amekia heard movement going on, on Carmen's end of the phone call. She was having slight discomfort but she managed to chuckle.

"Carmen. Relax. It was just one, and it could be a false alarm. Remember, I'm not even in my ninth month yet. Don't get yourself worked up. I'm not going nowhere until...ooooh shit. My water just broke," Amekia yelled into the phone.

"Denise, her water just broke. I need to get to her. Amekia stay right there, I'm on my way," Carmen frantically announced.

"You a bold face, bald headed ass lie. I'm calling an ambulance and going to the hospital," Amekia yelled and hung up the phone.

As carefully as she could, she walked to her room, grabbed her hospital bag, and cleaned herself up as much as she could. She picked up her phone and dialed 911 for an ambulance. They instructed for her to lay on the couch and keep the door unlocked, and they would be there soon. She did what they asked and laid on the couch. Another contraction rocked her body as she looked at the clock that sat on her living room wall to track how long the contraction lasted. Several minutes later, Amekia heard the door being swung open and she prepared to be bombarded by the EMTs.

"I'm in here," she called out so that they could follow her voice to find her.

"Oh my God. Are you okay?"

"Carmen. How the fuck you get here before the ambulance?" Amekia asked in shock.

"She broke every damn traffic law getting here," Denise stated as she took a seat on the couch opposite from Amekia. Two minutes later, EMT's arrived and asked her tons of questions as they loaded her onto the gurney.

"I'm gonna follow you, Amekia. I got your bag, and I'm gonna have Denise call Jade and Sasha so they can meet us there," Carmen yelled after Amekia as they placed her in the ambulance.

"Who should I call first?" Denise asked.

"Call Jade first. She's the baby's God mother."

***

For months, Jade had laid in her own filth. In the past two months, she had showered maybe a total of five times. The news that she received at the hospital had put her in a state of shock and caused her to shut everybody out. She was done with feeling sorry for herself and decided that she'd take the liberty of getting her shit together, by first taking a shower, and then cleaning her house.

Time and time again, she wanted to pick up the phone and call Darion, but her tears and the ache in her body stopped her from doing so.

As she was cleaning her kitchen, her music stopped playing and her phone began to ring. Looking at the caller ID, she noticed that it was Denise calling her. She knew something had to be up because, while they were friends with Denise, she never called any of them. She rushed to answer the phone.

"Hello?" She questioned.

"Bitch, get to Ellis. Your God daughter is about to be born," she heard Carmen yell through the phone.

"What? That's impossible, she still has another month."

"Well I'm following behind the ambulance right now. Get there now."

Jade turned her sink off and rushed to get ready to leave. She ran to her garage and climbed into her car, waiting for the door to raise up for her to leave out. Checking her rear-view mirror, making sure that she was clear to pull out, she saw Darion standing in her driveway. Her breath caught in her throat. She stopped her car and paused before she exited the car. Anger rose from the tips of her toes to the top of her hair follicles. She swung her car door open and stormed towards him, ready to attack him.

"What the fuck are you doing here?" Jade yelled. The tears freely falling from her eyes. As much as she tried to avoid him, she knew that this was something that needed to be done.

"I just wanted to talk to you, Jade. See how you're doing," he stated.

"You wanted to see how I was doing? Or you wanted to see if I got what you giving out?" She asked with her arms folded across her chest, trying her hardest to not knock his ass out.

His eyes grew big like saucers. There was no point in hiding his visit any longer. He asked, "Well do you?"

"How long have you known that you were HIV positive?" She asked with a shaky voice. She had just got to the point where she was out of denial and was going to accept her fate. She'd danced with fire, and now she just had to live with it.

"About two years now."

"What? Two years? Why the fuck are you just raw dogging females? I could fucking kill you, and I just might. You don't deserve to live. Get the fuck away from my house, and if I catch you anywhere near my house or my job, I will make good on what I said, and your son will be fatherless, too."

Jade was disgusted. How can someone who is knowingly HIV positive just go around spreading the virus. He was handing out death sentences, and then acting like he was so concerned. As Jade closed her car door, she screamed at the top of her lungs. The pain in her heart was indescribable. She banged her fists against the steering wheel as she let out all of her frustrations. Over the last two months, she'd contemplated suicide, but got rid of the thought once she realized that Amekia was going to be giving her a God baby. With that thought stuck in her mind, she dried her eyes and made her way to the hospital.

***

"When will she be able to push?" Carmen asked the doctor. The doctor had just finished giving Amekia a pelvic exam to determine how many centimeters she was. There was a machine to the right of Amekia's bed, tracking her contractions, an IV pole, and a table with a pitcher filled with ice.

"At this point she is only three centimeters. Her contractions weren't close or strong enough yet for her to push. Whenever baby is ready to come out, that's when she will be able to push. Right now, we just want to keep her comfortable," the doctor stated. He pulled Amekia's sheet down, tapped her on her leg, and walked out, leaving Amekia, Carmen, and Denise in the room.

Boom!

The door to Amekia's room banged against the wall as Jade made her entrance. She asked, "What did I miss?"

Amekia giggled and responded, "Nothing. Except your god daughter making my water break and don't want to come out."

Jade made her way over to Amekia's bed and touched her stomach. She was in awe as she rubbed Amekia's stomach. She felt the baby moving under her slight touch. Her tears appeared again as she took Amekia into a hug and thanked her for giving her reason to continue to live.

Amekia didn't know what she meant by that, but soon she would. Over the next few hours, the baby slowly made her way down Amekia's cervix. Nurses came in and out of the room, giving Amekia an epidural. Sasha hadn't returned anyone's calls but had finally showed up close to midnight when the doctor had come in to check how far Amekia had dilated. All eyes were on her as the tension in the room between the friends could be felt.

"You are nine centimeters, it's time to push," the doctor announced. The room became alive as everyone moved around the room to get ready for the arrival.

"I came at the perfect time then," Sasha stated with a weak smile on her face. Amekia didn't care at that moment what the fuck was going on with them. She was just glad they could put their differences aside and be there for her when it mattered most. They crowded around the top half of her body as the doctor and nurse instructed her when to push. An hour later, Amekia was exhausted and it seemed like her daughter didn't want to come out. The contractions were back to back but her baby wouldn't even crown.

"We'll give it a go again, but if she doesn't crown, we're gonna have to -"

Jade yelled, "Doc, I think I may see her head."

Going between Amekia's legs again, he saw that the baby's head was crowning. He got into position and instructed for Amekia to push with all of her might. Taking a deep breath, she placed her chin in her chest and pushed as hard as she could. Amekia saw Jade get excited and she knew that her daughter had finally stopped being stubborn and made her way into the world.

"One more push, and then she will be out. Push. Push. Push," the doctor coached. Amekia did what she was told, and then everything was still. The loud wails from the baby brought tears to all of her friends' eyes. And in that moment, she lived for it.

"She's here," Jade yelled excitedly.

The nurse held her up for Amekia to see, and Amekia couldn't help the tears from falling again. She asked, "What's her name mom?"

"Aziyah-Jae," Amekia beamed.

The nurses moved around, cleaning, weighing the baby, and cleaning Amekia up. The girls walked out of the room and waited in the waiting room in silence until they put Amekia in her room. An hour later, and she was settled in and the hospital staff gave them permission to say their goodbyes. One by one, they made their way inside of the room, making promises to see Amekia the next day. Sasha was the last to come into the room. The tension was so thick, if Amekia had a knife, she could've cut through it. She decided to be the first to talk.

"Thank you for coming. It means a lot. I'm sorry about what happened at the restaurant," she said. She felt the tears coming, but she didn't let them fall. She had done enough crying, and she just wanted her friendship back.

Sasha thought about the words that she chose to use before she responded. She said, "I had a long time to think about what happened, and when it happened, I was sorry. I thought that maybe I should have been a little more sensitive to your situation, and I shouldn't have said the things that I said. Now that I'm here in front of your face, I do not feel the same. I came for two things, to see the baby, and to give you this."

Sasha placed the envelope that she had in her hands on Amekia's lap. Amekia looked at it before she picked it up and began to remove the items. She asked, "What is this?"

"While I valued our friendship, I never thought I would feel such betrayal. Those, my friend, are custody papers. I know you was sleeping with Brandon behind my back, and I know that you was begging him to give your daughter a chance. So, I decided to make that happen. Me and my husband will be seeking custody of your baby. Checkmate, bitch," Sasha stated with a sly grin on her face. She walked out of the room without looking back, leaving Amekia staring at the papers in a state of shock. As she cried, she thought, *Is this for real?*

Mimi

Chapter One

Sasha felt a sense of relief as she walked out of the hospital, after serving Amekia a summons to appear in court. There was no way in hell, friend or not, she would allow another woman to have her husband's child without her doing something about it. In her mind, Amekia deserved it for the betrayal that she had bestowed upon Sasha. For several years, the affair between her husband and best friend had been going on behind her back, and she didn't have the slightest clue. Sure, she had suspicions that her husband was cheating, but never did she think he was having an affair with someone so close to her. While she was thinking about trying to bust her husband, it took for her to go out and cheat to find the truth.

Nasir was a Godsend when he shed light on Brandon and Amekia. He had text messages, phone records, pictures, and dates where they had met in public. She didn't know how he obtained that information, but when he presented it in exchange for her being with him, she knew she had to see what was going on. With every sheet of paper she looked through, her heart shattered in her chest. Brandon and Amekia made it seem like they hated each other's guts, so she never expected it. When Sasha had thought it over, it made perfect sense. There were so many times where she had heard stories of a best friend sleeping with the husband and making it seem like they hated each other. She just never thought it would happen to her. She thought her friendships were solid, but with this happening, she side-eyed every one of her friends. She questioned if they were really her friend or if they did the ultimate betrayal, as Amekia had done.

Sasha climbed into her car, and even though she was wearing a smirk on her face, she knew she was broken inside. She had confronted Amekia and now it was time to confront her husband. Before Sasha went to the hospital, she took her daughters over to Brandon's parents' house because she knew that it was going to be a huge blow up as soon as she made it home.

The day that Nasir gave her all of the evidence that she needed, Nasir had watched her from the door as she browsed each sheet of paper in tears. He knew she would never leave her husband and by him giving her the evidence, he figured that she would come running into his arms. It had the exact opposite effect, and she had been ignoring him. His calls and texts would go unanswered and he wanted to know what he did so wrong that she had to ignore him. The truth was that Sasha was so hurt that she was confused. She didn't know what she wanted to do, and she knew that if she kept in contact with Nasir, she would make decisions in that moment that could possibly hurt her or her girls in the long run. Ultimately, she had to make the best decision for her daughters.

Finally able to pull away from the hospital, her phone rang, and Jade's name appeared on the caller I.D. Sasha contemplated on answering, but didn't take too long, as she slid her finger across the screen to answer, instantly connecting the call to the Bluetooth.

"Yeah, Jade?" Sasha answered, paying attention to the road.

"Where did you go?" Jade asked.

"I have to go home and take care of something." Sasha was uninterested in their conversation and her tone said so. Her mind was dead set on her other girls disrespecting her in the same manner as Amekia.

"What the hell crawled up your ass?"

"Ask Amekia." Sasha stated and hung up the phone. She turned the phone off and blasted her music as she made her way home. When she had gotten there, she was expecting for

Brandon's car to be in the driveway, but it was not. *'He probably went to go see his love child. Mmmph!'* Sasha entered her home and stood at the door for a few moments. Her once happy home was now tumbling to the ground. Shaking her head, she went into her kitchen and poured herself a double shot of Crown Royal. She made a face, as the brown liquor burned her chest, as it went down.

Sasha took a seat at her kitchen table with another double shot, and powered her phone back on. Instantly, her phone went off, letting her know she had missed texts and phone calls, mostly from Jade. She would give Jade a call later. In this moment, she needed to find out where her loving husband was. As she moved her fingers swiftly across the screen to get to Brandon's name, her phone rang in her hand. It was Nasir. His call couldn't have come at a worse time. She decided answering the phone would put him on pause for the time being, so she answered.

"Hello, Nasir," she sighed into the phone.

"Thank God you answered! I have been trying to reach you since the day you left my house." He spoke through the phone, his voice laced with concern.

"Yeah, well since that day, I've been dealing with the shit that you put in front of me. I have a question for you though, was that done on purpose? Or did you really have good intentions behind it?"

Nasir paused. He wanted to make sure that what he said wouldn't put a damper on what he was trying to form with Sasha. He finally responded, "I had good intentions behind it. Now that I think about it, I should have done it in a better way. It was something that you needed to know, and if I knew and I didn't tell you, I didn't want you to get mad at me. There is something special between us, and I don't want to ruin that."

Sasha couldn't lie to herself, even if she wanted to. She

didn't doubt that there was something special, but this was coming all at the wrong time. She needed to focus on the shit show that she called her life, and not another relationship with another man.

She said, "Look, Nasir, I know that there is, but I need to take care of this. Our final court day is in two days, and I think that should be our focus right now. I have to prepare, and there is too much that is weighing heavy on my mind. We can revisit this conversation in a few days, okay?"

Nasir was impatient. He wasn't used to having such a hard time chasing a woman. In fact, he had never had to chase a woman. But there was something about Sasha that told him deep in his heart to just wait it out. So he agreed and allowed the conversation to end. For now.

Sasha looked down at her phone, which rested in her hand. She unlocked the phone and searched for Brandon's phone number. Then she heard keys at the door. Sitting patiently at the kitchen table, she waited until Brandon decided to make his way into the kitchen.

"Sasha!" She heard Brandon calling out to her.

"Kitchen," she replied plainly. His footsteps echoed off of the hardwood floors as he made his way to the kitchen. His scent greeted her first, and then his body. He walked up to her with a smile on his face and flowers in his hands. He planted a kiss on her forehead and placed the flowers in front of her.

"Why the long face?" Brandon asked as he grabbed a cup from the cabinet and poured himself some water, straight from the tap.

"Oh, could you tell?" Sasha responded. She grabbed the flowers from the table, walked to the garbage can, and threw them in there.

"What you do that for?"

"Is there something you want to tell me Brandon?" Her

anger was resurfacing.

Brandon looked on with confusion on his face. He didn't know what she knew. He didn't want to put himself in the position to where he admitted to something and he didn't know what she was hinting at to begin with. He looked dead in Sasha's eyes and said, "Not that I could think of. What's going on?"

The envelope that Nasir gave her rested inside of her purse. She walked to the living room, where her purse sat on the couch, and grabbed the envelope, making her way back to the kitchen. With a *plop*, the envelope landed on the counter in front of him. Brandon was further rendered into confusion as he cautiously eyed the envelope. Placing his glass next to the sink, he reached for the envelope, and slowly opened it. In front of his eyes was his relationship that he'd had with his wife's best friend, Amekia, on full display. There were pictures, text messages, meet up times. Everything that he had done with her was in front of his face.

"Let me explain," he mumbled.

"Let you explain what, Brandon? That you had an affair and a baby with my best friend right up under my nose?"

"She came onto me," he yelled.

"Oh wow. So because she came onto you, that gave you the right to entertain it? I am your wife, Brandon! Why didn't you come to me instead of entertaining her? That's if she did come on to you."

"I told her to get rid of the baby."

"And looky looky, she fucking had the fucking baby!" Sasha was at her peak with her anger. Her body trembled with each word that spilled from his mouth.

Brandon knew there was nothing that he could say at this point. He was caught, there was proof, and he didn't know what he could say to keep Sasha cool. His mouth opened and shut several times, trying to find the right words to say to her. He could see the hurt that she felt in her eyes. He knew he fucked up bad and there was nothing that he would be able to do or say to fix the situation. Not thinking about what he was going to say, he blurted, "First thing in the morning, I will go petition to give up my parenting rights."

Sasha couldn't believe him. The deed was done, but never in a million years did she think that he would say such a thing. She couldn't help the laughter that rumbled deep from her belly. She shook her head and said, "You bout the dumbest motherfucker. You will do no such thing. In fact, I served Amekia with custody papers right after she gave birth to your daughter."

Brandon's eyebrows raised. He surely heard Sasha wrong. She didn't just say that she was petitioning for them to get custody of the child that he had outside of his marriage. He said, "I'm sorry, what did you just say?"

"You heard every bit of what I just said. We go to court in a couple of weeks, so I expect for you to be prepared," Sasha said with malice. With one last look at her sorry husband, she walked out of the kitchen and left the house.

Chapter Two

After two days of being in the hospital, Amekia was relieved that she was going home. Jade was coming to pick her and Aziyah up from the hospital. After all the drama that had recently come up, she was grateful for her daughter. She looked everything like her no-good ass father, but her daughter was precious.

Amekia sat on the edge of the hospital bed, with all of her things packed. Next to her was the envelope that Sasha had given her, containing the custody papers. She had looked over those papers so much over the last two days that she could repeat every single word that was in the document. Amekia knew that Sasha handing her custody papers was to try and shake her up, but Amekia was stable, mentally and financially. There was absolutely nothing that a judge could do to award Sasha and Brandon custody.

"Hey, hey, hey," Jade shouted as she walked into the room. Amekia turned to look at her friend who looked better today than what she did a few days ago. A smile appeared on Amekia's face as she slowly stood up to take her friend into a tight hug.

"I'm so glad to see your face. I'm waiting for the nurse to come back with the discharge papers, and then we can blow this joint," Amekia said.

"Blow this joint? Girl, how old are you?" Jade asked with laughter.

"Oh, shut up! I can't wait to get home. I need real food, my hot water, and my bed."

"I don't blame you. Hospitals are supposed to make you feel comfortable while you are there. I mean not like hotel status, but damn. How is little Miss Aziyah doing?" Jade asked as she stood near the bassinet, looking down at the sleeping baby.

"She is so good. She has been sleeping her butt off, and I just want to wake her up and look into her beautiful eyes."

"Oh no, ma'am. While she sleep, you let her sleep, and you sleep, too. There is going to be plenty of sleepless nights, and you are going to want to get all the rest you can get," Jade spoke. She sat on the bed, brushing her fingers across the envelope. Amekia walked to the window and looked out of it.

"You know, Jade, I thought that I had found love so many times, but the way my heart feels about Aziyah, man. My heart feels so full now. If I would have known that it was going to feel like this, I would have been had a baby," Amekia stated with a smirk on her face.

Jade displayed a smile on her face. She was really happy for her friend, but the fact of the matter was that she needed to find out why Sasha was acting funny. Sasha told her to ask Amekia, so there she was, hoping that Amekia would be woman enough to tell her what the hell was going on. Jade looked at Amekia and asked, "Amekia, there is something that is going on with Sasha. When I asked her what was wrong with her, she told me to ask you."

At the mention of Sasha's name, Amekia turned in her direction and placed a scowl on her face. She said, "Sasha is not who the hell I want to talk about."

"That is our friend, Amekia and there is something going on with her. Lately, our sisterhood has slowly become undone, and I just want to figure out what is going on so that I can see what I could do to repair this."

"There is no fixing shit with her."

"What could have gone so wrong that y'all are acting like this with each other?"

"Jade, don't act like me and Sasha ain't been having a rift between us. If there is something wrong with her, then you need to be asking her that."

Jade looked down at the envelope and looked back at her friend. She ran her fingers across the thick envelope. She asked, "Amekia, what's in this envelope?"

Amekia looked at Jade and debated if she should tell Jade. Exhaling, Amekia sat on the hospital bed next to Jade. She picked up the envelope and took the papers from the inside of it. She handed them to Jade, and adverted her eyes to a corner of the room, as she tried to hold back the tears that threatened to fall from her eyes.

Jade looked over the papers in confusion. She asked, "Why is she taking you to court for custody? That is the dumbest, most asinine shit I've heard of. Is it that she wants to be the only one that has kids, so she would stoop so fucking low to try to take your daughter away from you? She's that fucking mad? The bitch is selfish!"

The tears dropped from Amekia's eyes, and she forced herself to make eye contact with Jade. She exhaled and said, "Brandon is Aziyah's father."

"What?" Jade screeched, causing Aziyah to jump from her sleep and proceed to wail.

"Dammit, Jade," Amekia yelled as she rushed to the bassinet to scoop Aziyah into her arms. As soon as she felt the warmth of her mother's skin, she immediately began to quiet down.

"I'm sorry. But what the fuck do you mean that she is Brandon's daughter? I am so confused."

"Give me some time, and I will explain it. I want to get home and get showered first."

Jade placed her hand against her forehead trying to process what she was just told. Being respectful, Jade dropped the subject. Moments later, the nurse came in with Amekia's discharge papers. Amekia was given after care instructions, and told to schedule an appointment for the baby in a few days for a follow up. With that, they were ready to go. In silence, they left out of the hospital. Amekia's mind wouldn't stop racing, and she barely heard anything that Jade was talking about.

When they arrived to Amekia's house, she noticed that her porch and front door was decorated. There was pink and white streamers, balloons, banners, and a door covering, welcoming her baby girl home. A smile came across her face as she climbed out of the car and stared. Looking over to Jade, she noticed that her friend was smiling hard as hell.

"What the hell do you have up your sleeve? You know damn well I just wanted to come home and relax," Amekia stated with a smile on her face.

"Yes, I know. Carmen and I just wanted to make sure that you and Aziyah were welcomed home properly."

"Oh, so Carmen is in on this, too?"

"Of course. I was with you at the hospital, how did you think the decorations happened?"

"Y'all are too much."

Amekia opened the back door and retrieved the car seat and baby bag that she received from the hospital. Together, they walked to the door and went inside. Her house was filled with pink and white balloons. Throughout the house there was pink and white decorations and the smell of food wafted throughout. Carmen and Denise were in the kitchen, putting the finishing touches on a bowl of macaroni salad, when they noticed Amekia and Jade had arrived.

"Welcome home," Carmen yelled.

"Wake my baby up, and it's gonna be me and you, hoe," Amekia warned with a smile on her face. She reached over and hugged Carmen, and then Denise.

They made their way into the living room and took turns with fawning over Aziyah. Amekia heard the distinct sound of the toilet flushing and she eyed her friends. They avoided eye contact with her, and she wondered who the hell else could be in her fucking house. The sink water turned on in the bathroom, and she eyed Jade.

"Jade, who the hell else is here? That bitch better not be here," Amekia said through clenched teeth.

Carmen looked between Amekia and Jade, and asked, "What bitch?"

"Sasha," Amekia stated almost in a snarl.

"What's the beef between y'all?" Carmen asked.

"Jade, she better the fuck not be here or she gonna be the one going to the hospital, and I'm going to jail."

"Amekia," came the sound from a stern voice. Her body stiffened at the sound of the familiar voice. It wasn't Sasha, and she was grateful for that because the Lord knew that she wasn't ready to leave her baby to go to jail. But if she had to, she would have.

"Why is she here?" Amekia asked, never turning to greet the guest.

Jade and Carmen looked at each other in confusion. Carmen spoke up and said, "We thought that it would be a good idea to have your mother here when you came home."

Amekia's body trembled in anger. She wasn't mad with her friends because she knew that their heart was in the right place. They had no idea why there was a rift in the mother and daughter relationship. How could they, when Amekia never told them what happened between the two women?

"You're not going to speak to me, Amekia?" her mother asked, only infuriating Amekia more.

"Mrs. Lewis, maybe this was a bad idea," Carmen spoke apologetically.

"No, this wasn't. My daughter has cut me off, and moved since the last I spoke to her, and I had no way of knowing how she was doing or the fact that I now have a granddaughter," Mrs. Lewis spoke sternly. She stood poised in the doorway of the living room, her hands folded in front of her. She wore a floral-patterned blue dress, six-inch black heels, and her hair was in a bone straight bob.

"Mama, you need to go. If I wanted you to know anything, I would have called and told you," Amekia snarled as she finally made eye contact with her mother.

"Girls, maybe you should leave and give us some time together. There are some things that me and my daughter need to talk about."

"No. Get your ass out of my house," Amekia yelled, standing from the couch, causing Aziyah to wake up in a screaming frenzy.

Jade, Denise, and Carmen looked on in shock as they stood with confusion. Mrs. Lewis looked at Amekia, and without a word, turned and walked away. Amekia didn't sit down until she heard the door close. Tears fell from her eyes as she picked up her daughter and calmed her down. Denise went to lock the door as Carmen and Jade sat down, wanting to know what was going on, but not wanting to ask the question.

"When my father was still alive, my mother was trying to convince him that I needed to get married. She wanted me to have an arranged marriage. Around that time, I wasn't the outspoken woman that I am today. I was timid and quiet, and my mother knew that I wasn't going to protest about the situation. She knew that I would just go with the flow. It was my father who was against it, and he spoke up for me every single time. One night, my father went out and she invited this man over. I didn't know who he was. She called me from my room, and told me to sit in the living room and wait for our guest to come back from the bathroom.

"She left from the living room, and moments later, a man

appeared. I was confused. I didn't know what was going on. He was an older man. Maybe in his forties. He was dressed in a suit, his goatee was lined to perfection, and his hair was cut short, almost bald. He looked like he was made of money. I asked him where my mother was and he responded that she was in her bedroom. He came over to the couch and sat next to me. At first, we sat quietly while we waited for my mother to return. He started to ask me questions. I became uneasy. Something wasn't sitting right with me." The more Amekia told her friends what happened between her and her mother, the more tears fell down her face.

"What happened?" Jade asked, holding back her own tears.

Moistening her lips with her tongue, Amekia began again. She said, "I tried to get up from the couch to see why it was taking my mother so long to get from her room. He grabbed me by my wrist, and I stopped right where I was. At this time, I was only nineteen. I wasn't sexually active yet, and I was innocent. There was everything in my gut telling me that there was something wrong with this situation, and that I should call for my mother for help. This man stood up behind me. He used his hands to rub the length of my body. And while my brain was screaming to stop this man, my body stood frozen. I could only stand there and let him. After some time, I felt his lips against my skin and I wanted to shout. I remember clocking out, my body was there but my mind wasn't. I felt him removing my dress. I remember him telling me that I was going to be his good little wife. I remember him forcing my body onto the couch. The tears fell from my eyes and he didn't care enough to stop.

"When I came back, he was laying on top of me, trying to force his way inside of me. I began screaming so loud that my voice became hoarse. I knew my mother heard me. She was still in the house. I screamed for her over and over again, while trying to fight that man off of me. He held my hands down, forced my legs open, and inserted himself inside of me. I begged for him to stop. He wouldn't. He just kept going, and telling me that if I obeyed him, and became his precious wife, I would have anything that I want, plus more.

"When he was done, I just laid there. He left. My mother came in the living room. Would you believe that she had a smile on her face? My throat was so raw from screaming for her to help me, and she shows up as soon as he leaves. She helped me from the couch, placed me in the tub, told me that I was to marry that man in two weeks, and to not mutter a word about it to my father. She told me that I had done well for myself. Two days later, I couldn't take walking around my father in a shell of myself and him not knowing what my mother had done. So while she was out, I told him. I told him every single thing. When she came home, he confronted her, and that was the same night he had a heart attack and died. I left the next day, and never looked back."

By the time Amekia was done telling her friends her story, they were all in tears. Besides Denise, she had been friends with them then, so they wondered why she had never mentioned this before. If they had known, they wouldn't have never invited her mother. They embraced Amekia with hugs, and apologized profusely. Amekia passed her daughter off to Carmen, and walked to the bathroom to get herself together. Today was supposed to be a happy day, and she wasn't going to let her mother ruin that.

"I'm sorry, y'all. I know y'all did this to make this a happy occasion. I'm done sulking, so let's have some fun," Amekia stated, when she came back from the bathroom.

Chapter Three

Carmen and Denise had gotten home a little after ten o'clock that night and what Amekia had revealed to them was still fresh on their minds, more so for Carmen than Denise. This was her best friend, and she had no idea something so terrible had happened. The thought made her sick to her stomach. She could only imagine how Amekia had felt. Carmen got in the shower and got ready for bed. She was starting a new job in the morning at a new doctor's office. The staff was predominately black, and she was looking forward to working with new patients. The time that she was out, she had missed her old ones.

"Are you ready for tomorrow?" Denise asked as she climbed into bed next to Carmen.

"Oh, yeah. I've been jobless for too long, and I just hope that this office isn't as messy as the other one. They literally drove me to almost kill myself," Carmen stated sadly.

Denise rubbed her back and said, "Yes, I know, bae, but you're here, and I will not allow that to happen again. If I could, I'd take down that whole office. And it sucks that the human resource people didn't do anything to help. Soon as you quit, they just gave up all communication."

"That's okay. When things happen like this and aren't taken care of properly, the company won't get extremely far. It's gonna take that one person who isn't gonna go for what they did to me and sue the hell out of them. That whole office is gonna go down the drain. Trust and believe me when I tell you. Mark was arrested. I hope it isn't as bad as it was when I left. Without him there, it should be good."

"Oh, I do believe it. Did you check to make sure that Amekia is okay?"

Carmen looked at Denise. There was a time when she

wouldn't have dared be caught with a woman. That all changed when Denise became her queen in shining armor. She had saved Carmen from jumping to her death off of the Craig Street Bridge. Denise not only saved her, she also made sure that she got home safely, and stayed the night with her. Some would say that Carmen was only with her because she had saved her, and she thought she owed Denise her life, but that was far from the truth. Carmen really fell for Denise, and as crazy as it may have sounded, she already knew that this was the person that she was supposed to be with for the rest of her life.

"I did while you were in the shower. She said that she was okay, and while the baby was sleeping, she was turning in for the night. I'm sure Jade stayed until Amekia fell asleep," Carmen responded.

"Have you spoken to Sasha?"

"Actually, I haven't seen or spoken to Sasha since Amekia gave birth. I'll call her on my break tomorrow. Her vibe has been off lately, and I don't know what is up with her."

"Seems like the whole group is having vibing issues. Maybe we should try to host a girl's night and invite everybody. We know that they aren't talking to one another so maybe it could work," Denise suggested.

"It may work. We can revisit this question, maybe Thursday. I have enough to worry about with this new job," Carmen replied. She reached over to Denise and placed a kiss on her lips. Carmen didn't think that what Denise suggested was a bad idea. She just knew that she would be pulling teeth and nails to get her girls in the same room.

***

Before Carmen knew it, Thursday had approached, and she didn't think that getting her girls together would be a good idea. Work was going smoothly for her, and surprisingly, she got along with all of her coworkers.

Carmen kept in the back of her mind that this wouldn't last long. She knew how low-down people could get from her last experience working in an office. It was almost time for Carmen to leave, but there was one more patient waiting on the doctor. She grabbed the file that was on the desk and walked to the patient's room. She knocked and then announced that she was coming in.

"Carmen?" She heard her name. Raising her head, Carmen recognized who had said her name.

"Sasha? What the hell?" Carmen responded in shock. She had no idea that Sasha brought her kids to that office. While she was shocked, she was delighted to see her friend.

"I didn't know you were working here?"

"I just started this week. I didn't know you brought Alexis and Aliana here. Hi, girls," Carmen stated with a smile.

"Hi, Auntie Carmen," Sasha's daughter's replied in unison.

"Well let's get this started. I see they are due for a physical. Let's start with height and weight, and move onto questions." Carmen completed her tasks and eventually left out of the room so that the doctor could go inside. When she saw Sasha, she forgot all about asking her over to her house on Saturday. *'I'll just catch her when she is leaving out,'* she thought to herself. She was getting ready to clock out anyhow, so she would just meet her at the door.

Ten minutes later, she saw Sasha approaching the door and cleared her throat. Sasha said, "I thought you would have been gone by now. I knew the girls were the last patients."

"Well, I waited because I wanted to ask you something. Would you mind coming over to my house this Saturday around nine? I miss you, and it seems like everybody is so divided."

"I don't know about that, Carmen."

"It's just going to be me you and Denise, I promise. Just for some wine and maybe some taco dip. I really miss you and want to catch up. To be honest, I miss all of us together. But if I have to see y'all separately, then I will do just that."

Sasha looked at Carmen, who was pleading her with her eyes. Carmen didn't do anything to her, so why should she be punishing her? Giving in, Sasha responded, "Okay, I'll come. I'll be there probably around nine-thirty. I got to make sure these monsters are in bed."

"Yes! That's what I'm talking about."

"Let me get them home. It's already passed dinner time, and they have school in the morning."

"Bye, girls. See you Saturday," Carmen said, waving at Sasha and the girls. She made her way to her car and climbed inside. Before starting her car, she sent a text to Jade and Amekia, asking them if they would show up at her house at eight on Saturday. They agreed. With a smile on her face, she made her way home to her girlfriend.

***

Carmen woke up Saturday morning full of energy. What she was preparing for could have turn into a disaster, but she was excited to have her girls all in one room, even if it only lasted for a little while. For the most part of the day, Carmen dragged Denise around, getting ready for the unexpected girls' night. Tacos were for dinner, and she was making mildly strong margaritas.

Everything was perfect by seven-thirty. To set the mood, Denise and Carmen had removed the couches and coffee table out of the living room, and placed the new floor pillows that they had purchased at Target. The tacos were done and the margaritas were chilling in the fridge. At eight o' clock on the dot, the doorbell rang. Carmen's heart hammered in her chest as she approached the door. On the other side stood Amekia.

"Thank you for asking your mom to baby sit. I just feel so bad leaving my baby," Amekia said as soon as she walked through the door. She was dressed in jeans and a t-shirt. A scarf was tied around her head, and her eyes looked tired. It had only been a few days since she'd been out of the hospital, and she looked drained.

"My mother needed some excitement in her life. Since Ashlyn and the kids left, she's just been by herself," Carmen responded.

Amekia made her way into the kitchen and greeted Denise. They hugged, and Amekia immediately went for a drink. "I have needed this so bad. Since my mother left, it felt like I was on edge. I've barely slept because I keep thinking that she is gonna pop up."

"Don't worry, she won't. Are you breast feeding? I didn't even think to ask before I made these drinks," Carmen asked as she hesitantly watched as Amekia guzzled her drink down.

Amekia swallowed the rest of her drink, and shook her head. She said, "No. Aziyah is having a hard time latching so the other day I decided to let her doctor know that. She does well on the bottle, so I'll just do Enfamil. But shit, my breasts have been killing me from not pumping the last three days. I was told to wear a tight bra, but shit, it seem like no bra was tight enough to stop the pain."

"I remember when Ashlyn went through that. Her reason to not breast feed was selfish though. She wanted to be able to drink and smoke," Carmen spoke with a roll of her eyes. Laughter erupted between the three, and then the doorbell rang. Carmen excused herself and went to answer the door.

Jade was standing on the opposite side of the door with a huge smile on her face. They embraced in a hug, and moved into the kitchen, where Denise already had a drink waiting for Jade.

"Oh, sweet Jesus, how I have missed seeing my girls in one room," Carmen stated as if she was going to cry.

"I'm just glad it's only us," Amekia stated.

Jade sipped her drink, and said, "Don't be like that, Amekia. Sasha isn't here to defend herself, and the shade isn't needed."

"Am I the only one that is out of the loop? I don't understand what is going on between you two. One minute, y'all good, and then the next, y'all at each other necks," Carmen retorted.

Jade shot a look at Amekia, and immediately, Amekia rolled her eyes. Having a baby by Sasha's husband was nothing that she was proud of. She could have stopped the affair before it even started, but it had gone on for years, and this was where she was. While she wasn't proud of the affair, she didn't regret it. She loved her daughter more than words could explain, and she was a big girl. She could deal with the consequences. In her mind, a part of her felt like Sasha needed to be humbled. Amekia felt that Sasha thought her life was so perfect that it was untouchable. Amekia taught her that it was very much so touchable, and she enjoyed teaching her that lesson. If that made her a bad friend, then so be it. She would eat that.

"Brandon is Aziyah's father, Carmen," Amekia blurted, stopping Carmen in her rant.

"McScuse me, bitch? What did you just say?" Carmen asked, turning her attention to Amekia.

"Look, Carmen, I have to live with that, and the fact that your bitch of a friend is trying to take custody of my daughter.

I don't need the scrutiny. I know what I did was wrong, but I have no regrets. Cause if I did, then that would mean that I regret having Aziyah, and I don't," Amekia stated with a shrug of her shoulders.

"Wait, back up for a second. She's trying to get custody?" Denise asked. Usually, she didn't jump in their conversations, but what she had just heard had her floored.

"The day that Sasha came up to the hospital, she wasn't there for good intentions. She served me court papers, saying that she wanted to gain full custody of Aziyah. Something about how I drink a lot, and being that her husband was the child's father, she felt like they should have full custody of the baby until I could attend AA meetings and prove that I would be a fit parent. I want to beat that bitch ass so bad, but knowing her petty ass, she would probably use that shit against me."

Jade's eyes bugged from her head as she almost spit her drink all over the kitchen. She said, "What? You didn't tell me that part."

"I didn't know until I got home from Aziyah's checkup. I took the time to read through the papers, and that funky, dog-headed bitch had the never to claim that I was an alcoholic. She got all that shit to say against me, but ain't saying how she running around here fucking on her client, who just so happens to be a well know Kingpin."

"Whattttt?" Carmen, Jade, and Denise yelled out in unison.

"How do you know that?" Jade asked.

"I have my ways of finding things out. Just like she found out that her husband has an outside child," Amekia said, and sipped on her drink. Carmen processed all of what was just said, and instantly regretted inviting Sasha. It was already reaching the time that Sasha was supposed to show up, and she didn't know what to do. Carmen knew that this was going to get ugly, and there wasn't anything that she could do.

"Jade, can you help me with bringing the coffee table back into the living room right quick? I forgot when we sit, we gonna need to place our cups somewhere," Carmen asked.

"Sure."

Jade and Carmen disappeared into the back of the house as worry etched across Carmen's face. She was just trying to get them all together so they could squash whatever beef anybody had. She now knew that this shit was running deeper than what she originally thought. When they arrived in the room, Carmen hurriedly closed the door behind them.

"Bitch, what you doing?" Jade asked.

"I think I did something fucked up," Carmen admitted.

"Listen, I can't deal with y'all bitches fucking up. What the fuck is wrong with y'all?"

"I invited Sasha."

Jade's mouth dropped as she made eye contact with Carmen. She knew that she didn't just hear what she thought she heard. Jade asked, "I'm sorry, you did what now?"

Carmen bounced from one leg to the other as if she had to pee, and her face screamed of worry. She responded, "You heard what the hell I said. I didn't know that all of this was going on. I just thought that they were going at it over the usual stuff."

Ding. Ding. Ding.

Carmen and Jade looked at each other as Carmen's heart sank to her ass. The bell went off again, putting fire under both Carmen and Jade's ass, causing them to rush out of the room. As they made their way down the hallway, Carmen saw Amekia approaching the door. Carmen felt her legs going weak as she felt like reality moved in slow motion. This was all a bad idea.

'This isn't my fault. If there was communication between

us then I would have known. Fuck it,' Carmen thought to herself. Her intentions were pure when she had listened to Denise, trying to get her girls together. If she had known how deep the beef went, this wouldn't have even happened.

"What the fuck are you doing here?" Carmen heard Amekia ask as she approached the door. The scowl on Amekia's face was etched deeply, and Sasha looked like she was a deer caught in headlights.

"Excuse me?" Sasha asked with a confused expression on her face. She looked between Amekia and Carmen. Settling her gaze on Carmen. Slowly she shook her head.

"Sasha, come in," Carmen stated. Jade looked on while she stood to the side, knowing damn well that shit was about to hit the fan. Denise stood in the kitchen, busying herself, pouring drinks that didn't need to be poured. Denise heard the doorbell while talking with Amekia, but her hands were full, and Amekia figured she would go answer the door.

Sasha thought about going in, and decided why the hell not. She'd come this far. She could deal with being around everybody, except Amekia, but if this was an opportunity for her to get under Amekia's skin, then she was for it. Staring at Amekia as she walked past, she made her way to the kitchen, where she greeted Denise. Carmen closed the door and turned her attention towards Amekia, who stared at Carmen.

"Why would you do this?" Amekia asked.

"I didn't know how deep y'all beef ran until tonight. If I would have known before, then I wouldn't have invited her," Carmen explained.

"So that makes this okay? I'm gone. Let your mom know I'm on my way to go get my baby."

Jade stepped in and said, "Y'all got a lot to talk about. I think you should stay."

"Are you kidding me? We have nothing to talk about, and

I can assure you that the slick shit she's tryna pull is gonna make me fuck her up. Besides the whole shit with Brandon, I can assure you that I valued our friendship. I regret that it was her husband, but shit happens, and I'm not about to sit around while she act all high and mighty," Amekia stated.

"As women, we need to learn to talk things through and hear each other out. There is nothing wrong with that. And it won't ever come to blows, because I'm not gonna let that happen. Amekia, please just stay. Y'all need to hear each other out, and figure out how to work through this," Jade tried to reason.

What was there for them to talk about? Sasha had made it noticeably clear what her intentions were. Amekia let her hand slip from the doorknob, which she didn't realize that she was holding onto so tightly that her knuckles were turning white. She exhaled, and tried to calm herself down. This was going to take a lot out of her, and she had to prepare herself mentally.

"Fine," she simply said, and turned away from the door. Jade and Carmen exhaled with relief as they all made their way to the kitchen. Denise was standing near the sink, cleaning up dishes, and Sasha had taken a seat at the table with her phone in her hand. The kitchen was quiet, a deathly eerie silence that killed each of them in a different way.

"So," Carmen started but was interrupted by Sasha.

"Let's address the elephant in the room. Shall we?" Sasha stated, and placed her purse on top of the table.

Amekia chortled under her breath, and crossed her legs.

"What elephant?" Carmen asked. She really didn't want to go there.

Sasha chuckled and said, "Carmen, don't act like you don't know. It's not flattering."

Carmen was taken aback at how Sasha spoke to her. She had done nothing to Sasha. But if that is the energy she was giving, she would give it right back.

Carmen stood up, placed her right hand on the table, her left on her hip, and leaned towards Sasha. She said, "I didn't find out the bullshit you and Amekia was going through until she mentioned it tonight. I get it. You're mad, but I ain't the one who is the cause of it, so save that. However, y'all both my friends. Y'all need to air some shit out, so why not do it now, while y'all can? And to be honest, this is ridiculous."

"Ridiculous?" Sasha exaggerated, like Soulja Boy did on *The Breakfast Club*. She continued, "This isn't just some nigga that I just so happened to be dating. Carmen, this is my husband we're talking about."

"Yes, I know who we talking about, but at the end of the day, you and Amekia have been friends for way too long for y'all to give it up like this," Carmen tried to reason.

"I can speak for myself. I tried talking to Sasha on many occasions since she served me those papers. Every call and text went unanswered. What more can I do? She think this is going to work in her favor, but it won't. And as a matter of fact, if you want to keep your marriage intact, you better stay from out of Nasir's bed. Out here fucking around on your husband, but worried about me...*pssh!* Don't you got all the nerve," Amekia stated as she leaned back in her seat. The room was silent as everyone took turns looking at each other.

Sasha's mouth hung agape as she couldn't, for the life of her, figure out how Amekia knew about Nasir. Sasha couldn't fix herself to produce a rebuttal. She grabbed her purse, slung it over her shoulder, and headed for the door.

Sasha was almost to the door when she doubled back and rushed Amekia. Friend or not, no one was going to disrespect her. The chair toppled over, and they both fell to the floor. Sasha's bag slid across the floor and landed at Denise's feet. Sasha sat on top of Amekia, pulling at her hair and slapping her. Jade, Denise, and Carmen looked on in shock, not knowing what to do. Amekia bucked her hips, trying to get Sasha off of her. With her last buck, Sasha flew over Amekia's head and crashed into the wall, headfirst, causing her to feel dazed. Amekia got up and stood over Sasha, wrapping her hand around her hair.

"See, bitch, I wasn't gonna take it this far, but you had to be the one to do it," Amekia yelled as she used her left hand to pull Sasha's head back and swung with her right, connecting blows to her face. She immediately caused Sasha's lips to split and leak blood. Jade had seen enough, and decided to grab Amekia. She paused when she realized that if she got in the middle, at any moment her skin could be broken, leaking her own tainted blood onto one of her friends. That thought alone made her sick to her stomach.

Jade turned to Carmen and said, "Can you break them up?"

"You was just about to do it, why didn't you?" Carmen asked as she tried to pull her eyes from her friends.

They were going at it like two women in the street. From the outside looking in, one would have thought that they had never known each other. Jade and Carmen went back and forth about who was going to break them up. Denise rolled her eyes and grabbed Amekia by the waist, pulling her off of Sasha. Amekia still had a good chunk of Sasha's hair in her hand as Denise pulled her, so Sasha was being dragged as Denise pulled Amekia.

"Bitch, you know you can't fight, so why would you even want to try it with me? Huh?" Amekia yelled as she kept swinging on Sasha.

"Let me go, bitch! Let me go and I'ma show yo' ass how much I can't fight," Sasha yelled. Her head was in an awkward position and blood was leaking from her face. Carmen finally jumped in to help Denise by prying Amekia's fingers from Sasha's hair.

Jade cried, "Come on, y'all, stop. We all friends, and this ain't the way to solve the issue at hand."

Carmen finally managed to pull Amekia's fingers from Sasha's hair and help Sasha from the ground. Both Amekia and Sasha were out of breath and glaring at each other as if they wanted to kill each other.

Sasha looked around the room at her friends and felt betrayed. She said, "Y'all knew this shit was going to happen, but yet and still, Carmen, you convinced me to stay. If I have to go through the rest of my life without speaking to you bitches, I'll be just fine."

Carmen looked at Sasha in shock. She pointed her finger at Sasha and said, "You attacked her first. That wasn't on us. Yes, I was the one who invited you and convinced you to stay, but you swung on her first. I thought y'all could be women enough to talk this shit through, but I was wrong. You can blame us for everything else, but you tried to fight her first."

Amekia used her index finger to wipe blood from the corner of her mouth. She looked at the women in the room and threw her hands up. She said, "You know what, I'm done with this shit. I already apologized, and I won't continuously do it. I was not the only one involved in this, and I for damn sure wish to not be the only one that is continuously getting penalized for this shit."

Amekia shook Denise off of her shoulder and grabbed her purse off of the table. She was going to drive to Carmen's mother's house and get her baby. The tears fell from her eyes as she visualized her daughter's face in her mind. She was the most precious thing in this world, and so innocent. She would go to the ends of this earth to protect her, and she wouldn't let anyone get in her way.

Mimi

Chapter Four

When Sasha and Amekia left, Denise, Jade, and Carmen stood around trying to process what had just happened. When they were younger, they made a vow to always have each other backs, and fight the bitches that hated on them, but never were they supposed to put their hands on each other. That vow got them well into adulthood, until Sasha thought it was okay to do so. Slowly, the three women began to clean up the kitchen, picking up the toppled over chairs along the way. They cleaned in silence for fifteen minutes before retreating to the living room to have much needed drinks.

Jade was the first to speak, saying, "I can't believe that just happened."

"We feel the same. I can't believe that Sasha tried to play victim when she was the one who swung first," Carmen stated.

"I get why Sasha is furious. The baby is innocent in this, but Sasha needs to be angry with Brandon as well," Denise stated.

Jade and Carmen nodded their heads in agreement. Jade said, "We don't know how Sasha is dealing with Brandon. For all we know, she could have either taken her girls and left, or he could be the one behind Sasha trying to get custody of Aziyah."

"Do you think Sasha and Brandon will get custody of her?" Carmen asked. Amekia had just become a parent. To their knowledge, Amekia was a good mother. The circumstances are just a tad bit fucked up.

"Sasha isn't the other parent. She's a damn good lawyer, but if Brandon gives up his parenting rights, I think the judge would throw the case out. Sasha gotta let them folks know that she feels like the baby is either being neglected or abused under Amekia's care to get it. We all know that Amekia isn't doing that. We know that she feels bad about the situation, but making those allegations would have to come with proof. I'm quite sure if Sasha made those allegations, CPS would be all over it, and watching Amekia like a hawk. Sasha is opening Pandora's Box by doing so. Amekia is a mother now, she's no longer just looking out for herself. She is going to protect her daughter. If Brandon don't know now that his wife is cheating, Amekia will let him know. You know that girl don't hold water, especially if she's the one hurting," Jade stated.

The room grew silent as all three women had different thoughts. Denise partly took Sasha's side. What Amekia did was wrong. Who knew how they were having an affair? Sasha was the victim, whether Carmen liked it or not. Granted, she was cheating on her husband, but she speculated that he was cheating, and that alone gave her the courage to slip into another man's arms.

Carmen felt for Sasha, she truly did. But she couldn't help but for her heart to go out to Amekia. What Amekia did was wrong, but did she really deserve Sasha trying to get custody of her daughter? Aziyah was in great hands, and what Jade had said rang true. Sasha had no leverage except that she was a good lawyer. For the remainder of the night, the three women sipped on their drinks and spoke their thoughts on this situation.

***

Sasha sat at her vanity, using her make up wipes to wipe the blood from her face. A bruise was slowly starting to show under her right eye, her nose was swollen, and her bottom lip looked like she had been stung by a bee. She was still in disbelief at what had happened at Carmen's house. She knew that she was in the wrong for swinging at Amekia. Dead wrong.

But what was she supposed to do? Actually sit there and talk to her ex best friend about her sleeping with her husband. Brandon and Amekia were both wrong. Sasha looked at herself in the mirror and watched as the tears cascaded from her eyes. She wondered what she did to them that warranted this kind of betrayal. She was hurt beyond measures, more than she was angry. She would never let anyone know that, though.

Sasha finished wiping the blood from her face and looked at herself once again, horrified by how she looked. Her hair was all over her head, despite trying to smooth it down as she made her way home. Thank God her kids were still away. She didn't know what she would have done if they saw her the way she was. Placing her arms on the top of her vanity, she rested her head on top of her arms. She sniffled as she tried to stop the tears, but they were relentless. Her mind spun at her options and what she should be doing in this position. She smelled him before she felt him put his hand on her shoulder.

"What do you want?" she asked, her voice icy. Her head remained on her arms.

"Sasha, I heard when you came in and wanted to give you your space, but baby, I can hear you crying all the way downstairs. Tell me what you want me to do to fix this. Even if you don't believe me, I never meant for this to happen," Brandon expressed, kneeling down next to her. He pulled at her arms trying to get her to look at him, but she wouldn't budge. Her face was horrendous, and she didn't want him to see that his side piece got the best of her.

"You didn't mean for it to happen, or you didn't mean for you and her to get caught?" she asked, finally lifting her head from the table. His mouth dropped in horror at the sight of his wife. He was rendered speechless.

"What the fuck happened to your face?" he managed to ask.

"Your side piece is what happened to my face. Carmen invited me over and, like a fool, I went. I didn't think that that broke bitch would be there, and when I found out, I thought that I could just get through a couple of hours and then leave. But then the bitch snuck me and-"

"She did what?" Brandon yelled. Sure she lied. She wasn't going to let him know that she swung first, and missed, causing Amekia to beat her down like a dog, like she had been the one to have slept with Amekia's husband. Brandon was pacing back and forth behind her. She watched him through the mirror.

"I said she snuck me," Sasha stated again.

"What did your other friends do? Cause if you look like that, then I'm sure that they didn't do much to stop it."

"You know what, just drop it. Because if you wouldn't have slept with Amekia, this wouldn't even be happening."

Brandon stopped pacing behind her, and they eyed each other through the mirror. He knew she was right, but he didn't want her to keep bringing that up. He would be willing to do anything for her to drop it, but there was a baby involved. He ran his hand down his face and looked at his watch.

"I'm going to fix this," Brandon stated as he made his way out of the room.

"Don't bother. I'm done."

"What?" Brandon yelled, pausing in his footsteps. He didn't think that she would take it that far.

"Brandon, you might as well start packing your shit and looking for an apartment. I will not tolerate the man that I married cheating, and move on like it was nothing," Sasha said as she grabbed her paddle brush from her vanity and began to do her hair.

"Sasha, please. If you would just hear me out," Brandon begged.

"Hear you out? You lucky that you are even still in my presence. Hear you out for what? To tell me that this was a mistake and that you love me and you don't want to lose me and the girls? Tuh! Brandon, I have done everything in my power to make sure that you and the girls were taken care of and loved. And this is the thanks I get."

Brandon scrunched his face up. He said, "Yes, you loved us, but where were you when your man... no, no, no, husband needed to be loved on. For the past few months, you have neglected me sexually, and when I slipped up and had sex with your best friend, I'm the bad guy."

Sasha dropped her brush on top of the dresser and looked at Brandon. *'Does this fool really think that anything he just said made any sense?'* Sasha thought to herself. She couldn't stop the chuckle that escaped from her lips.

She said, "Are you serious right now? You are the reason why I didn't have sex with you. I been saw your moves being funny, and I knew you were doing something. But you were a crafty motherfucker and you hid that shit perfectly. I would have never thought that you and Amekia would actually do this shit to me. But y'all did. I handled her, and now I need to handle you. Get your shit together so that you can move out of my house. You could go live with her and your child 'cause, Brandon, I am so done."

Brandon watched Sasha as she picked up her brush again and continued to do her hair. He knew that she was right, but her putting him out was wrong. He was wrong for cheating, but like he had mentioned, what was he supposed to do? He scrunched his face up, grabbed his car keys, and left the house. His destination was Amekia's house. He hadn't seen the baby since she had her, and he needed to see with his own eyes that she was his daughter.

***

Amekia's block was quiet as Brandon pulled up into her driveway. Her car was there, along with another one. He didn't recognize the car, so he was grateful that it wasn't one of their friends. Brandon shut his car off and stared at Amekia's house. He had spent a lot of good times there. When he had needed somebody to listen to him, when his wife was too busy, he went to Amekia. When he wanted sex, he went to Amekia. When he just wanted to chill and have a beer, he went to Amekia. She had really been his peace. At one time, he even thought about leaving Sasha to be with Amekia. He loved Sasha with everything in him, but he also loved Amekia. He wouldn't ever say that out loud, but that didn't change the fact that he did.

Sighing, he got out of his car and slammed the door shut. There was a light on upstairs, most likely the stair light. The first floor was lit up like it was six in the evening, instead of almost eleven at night. He walked up the four steps that led up to her front door, and paused before he pressed his finger against the doorbell. Resting his forearm against the door frame, he slightly shook his head. There wasn't a reason as to why he should be there, but there he was. The sound of the door being unlocked brought him back to reality, and he stood up straight. His heart started pounding in his chest as he became nervous.

Amekia's brown doe eyes looked up at him in surprise. She had mascara running from her eyes, a telltale of her crying. His heart melted into his chest as he took her in. She was still in the clothes that she must have worn over to Carmen's house. There was blood on her clothes. She asked, "Why are you here?"

Brandon's words were caught in his throat. He missed her.

He didn't realize it until his eyes landed on her. He said, "I um. I came because I heard what happened between you and Sasha. Why would you attack her?"

"What?" Amekia asked. She was flabbergasted.

"Can I come in? Your block is quiet and I don't want to have this conversation out here, in case it gets loud. By the way you just responded, I can tell it will."

"Absolutely not," she yelled.

"Well can you let me in so I can see my daughter?" he asked. He didn't want to pull that card, but if it got them to have that conversation inside, he was going to do it. Brandon knew that she would allow it. All she wanted was for him to be there for his daughter.

"I know I'm gonna regret this, but I'm not bitter, so come on," Amekia spoke as she rolled her eyes. She wasn't going to hide his child from him. She wanted him to know her, just like he knew his two other kids. They entered into the living room, where Brandon noticed a man sitting on the couch. He looked comfortable with a beer in his hand and his right foot on top of the coffee table.

"Who the hell is this?" Brandon asked. He would be lying if he said that he didn't feel intimidated by the presence of another man in her home, around his child. Shit, for all he knew, Amekia was probably sleeping with him while he was sleeping with her, and he could have been the father of her child.

"Why does it matter who the hell is in my house? You're not my man, Brandon," Amekia seethed.

"Were you fucking him while you were fucking me? Is that his child, Amekia?" Brandon asked while his eyes were still trained on the man on the couch. When Brandon had walked in, the man sat there and sipped his beer, not paying them any attention. But the sound of this jealous man questioning his side piece made him chuckle.

Amekia exhaled loudly. This was not what she wanted to have to deal with after she had just finished putting the paws on her ex-best friend. She said, "Not that I have to do this, but, Brandon, this is my brother, Nasir. Nasir, this is Aziyah's father. Sadly."

Brandon instantly fixed his face from a scowl into one that looked like he had egg on his face. Nasir stood from the couch with a smug look on his face and his hand outstretched towards Brandon. Nasir said, "Nice to put a face to the name."

Brandon shook his hand but turned his attention back to Amekia. He stated, "You never mentioned that you had a brother."

"He was out of the house before I even became friends with Sasha, and we haven't always had the best relationship, so I never talked about him," Amekia shrugged, which was somewhat true.

"Why does your name sound so familiar?" Brandon asked trying to figure out where he'd heard the name.

"Could be because I share my name with a lot of people, including the dopest Queensbridge rapper, Nas," Nasir chuckled.

"Could be. Say, man, did you just get out of jail?"

Amekia's eyes bugged from her head. She gasped and said, "Brandon."

"Nah, Mekia. It's cool. In fact, I did. I got this bomb ass lawyer working on my case, and she a dime. Mekia hooked me up with her. She told me that she could help me get out, and dammit, she did," Nasir spoke with a smirk on his face.

"That would be my wife," Brandon stated, slightly bruised at the fact that this man was lusting over his wife.

"Wait! You're married and you got a baby with my sister.

Mekia, you didn't tell me that he was married," Nasir stated, focusing his attention now on his sister.

She folded her arms across her chest as she looked at her brother. She said, "Nasir, it's time for you to leave. What I do is none of your business."

"Okay. I'll go. Give my niece a kiss for me. I'll be by tomorrow with a bunch of things for her room," Nasir responded while placing a kiss on top of her forehead. Still with a smirk on his face, he left the house.

Once he was gone, Brandon began to speak. "Look, I'm sorry about that."

"Yeah, whatever. Let me go get Aziyah."

"Wait, before you go, what happened between you and Sasha?" he asked. He knew he was pushing it but he had to know.

"What did she tell you? Cause whatever she told you, it ain't go down like that?"

"She said you sneaked her."

Amekia looked dead in his face and laughed. She laughed so hard she doubled over and held her stomach. She managed to get out, "What? She going around saying that I sneaked her when she swung first, and I tapped that ass. She wanted to be brave and try me first, but going around talking like I'm the bully."

Brandon looked at Amekia. He knew she was telling the truth, and wondered why Sasha told him that Amekia was the aggressor. He put that to the back of his mind, and decided that he would deal with that later. He asked, "Can you go get her. After I see her, then I will be on my way."

Amekia chuckled as she walked towards her daughter's room. She was sleeping in her crib peacefully, and she didn't want to disturb her. She took a moment to look into her crib and admire the gorgeous baby that she had brought into this world. Amekia wanted nothing more than to have her daughter live a drama free life. She didn't get that chance, but she would move mountains to make sure that her daughter didn't live the life that she lived.

"She's beautiful, Amekia," she heard Brandon say in a whisper. She was so into her baby that she didn't hear him come inside of the room. She quickly wiped the tears from her face. She smiled lightly and continued to look on while her daughter slept.

"Thank you," she responded in a whisper.

"She looks just like you, but she got my lips, nose, and definitely my big ass ears," he chuckled. Brandon adverted his attention to Amekia. He continued, "I should have been there when you gave birth to her. There is a lot of things that I should have done that I didn't because of what I thought Sasha was going to do behind this."

"She's threatening to take me to court for full custody, Brandon," Amekia stated. Her eyes were still on her daughter.

"What?" he asked. It was his turn to be flabbergasted. He didn't know that that's what she was doing.

"Yeah. She served me after I pushed my baby out," Amekia stated as she wiped the fresh tears that fell from her eyes. Brandon felt bad. He had no idea that Sasha was doing all of this. He didn't make up his mind right away, but he knew that once he had gotten the chance to see his child, he would have no doubt that he was going to take care of his daughter. Just like now, he knew that he wasn't going to abandon Aziyah. She was gorgeous.

"I'm sorry that Sasha is making this shit hard for you. I had no idea that she went and did this. Hell, I've barely been able to speak with her since the cat was let out of the bag," he said as he rubbed her shoulders to comfort her.

"Look, Brandon, I appreciate you stopping by to see her,

but if you gonna be one of those niggas who would flaunt his kids with his wife in public, and love on the one from the mistress in private, then you might as well let me fight this fight against Sasha by myself. I didn't make Aziyah alone, but I damn sure brought her into this world alone, and I don't mind taking care of her alone," Amekia grabbed the blanket that was laying across her daughter's leg and pulled it up to her chest. Aziyah was going to be waking up in another hour, and she wanted to shower and get some rest before she did. Sighing, Amekia grabbed the baby monitor and made her way back to the living room. Brandon followed.

"Amekia, I'm sorry for handling the situation the way that I handled it. Instead of blowing up and acting childish about it, I should have just had a sit down with you and spoke to you. I'm sorry that Sasha has this dumb ass idea in her head, and I will do everything in my power to make things right." What Brandon said sounded good. But Amekia was all about actions, because a nigga will say whatever sounds good in the moment and never follow through.

Amekia folded her arms across her chest and moistened her lips with her tongue. She bent her head upwards to look at Brandon in his eyes. She needed him to know how serious she was when she spoke him. She said, "Brandon, you know damn well that what you saying sounds good, but I'm all about that action. And you know this. So instead of saying it, you gonna have to prove it to me. Hell, you gonna have to prove it to your daughter before me, and you might as well start now if that's how you talking."

A smirk spread across Brandon's face. He had missed the feistiness that exuded from Amekia. He walked closer to Amekia and wrapped his arms around her neck and kissed the top of her forehead. She wanted to push him away but it was just easier if she stayed there, inhaling the faint sent of his Irish

Spring soap. After a minute or two, he finally said, "I got you."

Realizing that she was being sucked into almost making the situation worse, she pushed away from him and said, "Look, maybe you should leave. I know Aziyah gonna be up in an hour, and I need to shower and at least relax a little bit before she does."

"Nah. I'm not going nowhere. Go shower. I got Aziyah when she get up, if that's okay with you," Brandon stated. She was right, he had to show and prove, and he was going to start by staying the night to bond with his baby girl. He was the cause of this situation, just as much as Amekia was, and he was going to stick to his word to step up, and show and prove.

Amekia was skeptical. She battled with herself and whether she should let him stay or not. She finally answered, "That's fine. As long as you pull that air mattress out of the closet, fill it up in the living room, and drag it into her room. Good night, Brandon."

Brandon's mouth fell open as he watched Amekia sashay away. He couldn't help but to admire her ass and hips. Aziyah did her body good. He was still trying to get in her good graces, so he didn't comment. However, he did say, "That's how you gonna do me?"

When Amekia made it to her room, she eyed him up and down, and without another word, she walked inside her room and shut the door behind her. She was going to enjoy her first night "without" her daughter.

The first thing she did was strip out of her clothes, throwing them inside of the hamper. She made sure the shower water was hot enough for her liking, and climbed in. She placed her whole body under the shower head as the water soothed her aching muscles. It had been years since she fought, and she would go another few years if she didn't have to feel that pain again. When she was done, she lightly patted her skin dry with her towel and put on her pad covered panties before she sat down on the toilet to moisturize her skin with Dr. Teal's Milk and Honey lotion. A towel sat on top of her head with her wet hair wrapped inside of it. She took it off and decided to let her hair air dry as she dressed in black stretch shorts and a sports bra.

Amekia cleaned up her bathroom and climbed into her bed. Picking up her remote, she quickly placed it down. She wasn't in the mood to watch T.V. Going inside of her nightstand table drawer, she pulled out her Kindle, plugged it into the charger, and scrolled through the many books that she had downloaded on to it. She settled on a book by one of her favorite authors from Lock Down Publications. She had been desperately waiting for this book to drop and was glad that she finally had the chance to read it. *'Thank God Brandon decided to stay. I needed this time to myself,'* Amekia thought to herself. Before getting comfortable under the covers, Amekia turned on the air conditioner and relaxed until she fell asleep.

Mimi

Chapter Five

Jade woke up the next day. Her body was weak and she had little energy. The little bit of sun that was shining into her bedroom caused her to slam her eyes shut and wish for the pain that her body was going through, to go away. She wondered how long it would be before she stopped feeling these aches and pains. The sound of her alarm irritated her, as she reached for her phone to dismiss the alarm. Finally, she opened her eyes and talked herself out of the bed. Her stomach turned as she sat on the edge of the bed, her head spinning. She willed herself to think about anything other than how she was feeling. Her thoughts landing on what happened the previous night with her best friends.

Jade stood from the bed, taking one step off of the white carpet that her bed sat on top of. The cold sensation pushed her thoughts out of her mind, and she went full speed to the bathroom. The bile rose in her throat, burning it in the process. Her nose ran with snot and her eyes watered with tears. *'There is no way that this is going to be the rest of my life,'* Jade thought.

When there was nothing left to come from her stomach, she leaned against the wall and took deep breaths. Her knees were drawn into her chest, as her elbows rested on her knees, and her head in her hands.

"Lord, I don't know why you gave me this disease, but I can't take it. I'm ready to call this the end, but I know that you do things for a reason. Please Lord, just take this pain away," Jade cried out loud.

The cold from the tiled floor soothed the back of her legs. She managed to get on her hands and knees and crawl to the bathroom sink. Reaching up towards the sink, she pulled herself up and ran the water. Cold water splashed into her hands as she scooped it up and coated her face with it. For just a few minutes, relief washed over her body. The cold water felt good.

Feeling a little dizziness, Jade walked back to her bedroom with a cold wash rag and laid down with it on her forehead. There was no way possible that she was going to make it in to work. Grabbing her phone, she placed a call to the school district she worked for. She let them know that she wouldn't be in for that day and wished to use her sick time.

"In fact, I don't think I'll be in tomorrow, either. I know this is last moment, but I'm not at all feeling well, and I would feel horrible if it was the flu and I passed it along to anyone. I'll just use a week and a half of my sick time," Jade rambled, trying to keep her eyes open.

"I do apologize, Miss Rios. Make sure that you have your doctor's note when you come back," the sweet receptionist said through the phone. Jade thanked the woman and allowed her eyes to close. Her thoughts swirled around in her head as she wondered about what she would put on her stomach to at least stop the pains.

The next time Jade opened her eyes, the sun had moved across the sky and her room was a tad bit darker than earlier. Grabbing her cell phone, she checked the time. It was damn near two in the afternoon. She sat up, thinking that that was the best sleep she had ever had. She felt refreshed. Climbing out of the bed, Jade went to the bathroom and hopped in the shower.

The sound of shattering glass caused her to jump just as she was about to wash the soap from her body. She turned the water off and grabbed her towel, slowly making her way to check out the sound. As she crept down her hallway, with her back pressed against the wall, she wished that she had a gun.

Jade strained her ears to see if she heard anything else to indicate where the noise had come from. The only thing that she heard was the sound of her heart beating in her ears.

Creeping further along the wall, she finally reached the stairs. Silently she went down the stairs and maneuvered to the living room. Just as she suspected, that's where the shattered glass was. Her living room window that overlooked her side porch was broken all over the floor. Making sure that no one was in her home, she made her way further into the living room and looked at the damage. *'Why the fuck this shit gotta happen to me?'* Jade thought to herself.

Walking to the front door, she peeked out of the glass next to her door to see if there was anything unusual. There was a car, sitting outside of her house running. She would have just written it off as somebody there for one of her neighbors if she didn't recognize the person behind the wheel. Tanya was sitting behind the wheel of a car, with a smirk on her face. Jade stepped onto her porch to see if Tanya had something she wanted to say. Tanya simply stuck her middle finger up and sped off, leaving Jade pissed off to the max.

Turning on her heels, Jade stormed into her house, closing, and locking the door behind her. She rushed to her bedroom and retrieved her phone from the spot it was laying in on her bed. Jade hadn't spoken to Darion since the day he was in her driveway, when Amekia had given birth. She couldn't help but wonder why Tanya was acting like a bitter, mad woman. Jade found the number that she was looking for and hit the dial button. Only for the number to ring twice and go to voicemail. Frustrated, she slammed the phone onto the bed. Wasting her time was something that Jade was not about to do. She had a few days off and she wanted to enjoy them, while getting her mental headspace together.

Dressing quickly, Jade's first stop was going to be to

Home Depot. She needed to board up her windows until she could get someone to come out and fix them. As she shopped, her phone rang. She looked at the caller I.D. and rolled her eyes when she noticed that it was Sasha calling. She loved Sasha, she truly did, but she didn't approve of the way she acted at Carmen's house.

"Hello," Jade answered. She heard movement on the other side of the phone, and she knew Sasha was about to hang up.

"Jade?" Sasha questioned.

"That's who you called. What's up?" Jade asked as she headed to the checkout line.

"Look, I really need somebody to talk to and you're the only one that I feel like isn't turning against me. Can I stop by later on, when I'm done with work?" Sasha asked, holding her breath.

"Let me be clear. Carmen and Denise ain't did shit to you. They didn't even know what was going on until I told them right when you showed up. Don't do Carmen that way. To answer your question, yes you can. I have something I need to take care of when I get home, so give me about two to three hours, and give me a ring."

"You're right. I'm going to call Carmen and apologize to her. I'll let you go. See you soon," Sasha said as she hung up.

Jade slid her phone into her back pocket as she loaded her items into her car. She had help from an employee to attach the pieces of plywood to the top of her car. Jade stopped at a local Taco Bell, and then headed home. She was thankful that her living room faced the side of her house and the windows were protected by a screened in porch that always stayed locked.

Jade was busy taking the plywood off of her car, she didn't notice Darion walk up on her. He stepped next to her and said, "Let me help you with that."

"Arrgh! Darion, what the fuck are you doing here?" Jade questioned, squinting her eyes at him.

"You called me."

With her hands on her hips, she said, "So, because I called you, that gives you the right to just show up? Why didn't you just call me back?"

"When I noticed that you called, my phone was dying. I don't have my car charger with me, so I thought that it would be okay for me to stop by," Darion explained as he placed the plywood over the top his head and carried it to her front door.

"I can't believe you thought it was okay to drag your trifling ass on over here," Jade huffed. She was glad he was there. Instead of telling him about his girlfriend over the phone, she felt better that she could curse his ass out about it in person. Walking around Darion, she unlocked the door and let him in.

"Where do you want these? What do you need them for anyway?"

"In the living room. Your dusty ass girlfriend thought it was a good idea to break my windows. Her dumb ass picked my lock on my screened in porch and took it upon herself to indeed have an ass whooping waiting on her ass the next time I see her."

Darion made his way into the living room and placed the plywood against the wall. He looked at all of the glass that was on the floor and doubted that it had anything to do with Tanya. He asked, "How do you know it was her?"

Jade placed her hands on her hips, once again, and tilted her head to the side. She said, "So you think I'm just out here causing drama for myself? Nah, playboy, that was you when you decided that your nut ass wanted to cheat on that crazy bitch with me."

"If you got some nails and a hammer around, I can fix this

for you." It was the least he could do. He unintentionally ruined her life. When he had unprotected sex with Jade, he knew he was wrong for going in her raw dog, knowing his positive HIV status. He knew he was wrong, but the sight of her wet pussy was calling his name. Tanya wasn't as wet as Jade, and he knew that he had to have it. It had been years since he touched something so wet and gushy, and the excitement of it all caused his better judgment to go out of the window. Darion watched as Jade walked out of the living room to go get the items that he requested.

"In a way, I'm glad you're here. I was too livid with you to speak with you the last time I saw you. I've made my peace with the hand you dealt me, so I'm more than ready to give you a peace of my mind. So before you board them windows, have a fucking seat," Jade stated as she came back into the living room. He sat on one end of the couch, while Jade sat all the way on the other end.

Jade's heart thumped in her chest as she tried to figure out what she was going to say. If she didn't love her freedom, she would have slid into her kitchen, grabbed the biggest kitchen knife that she had, and caused a bloody scene that Jason Voorhees would have been proud of.

"Jade, I'm sorry," Darion said, sulking, with his chin tucked into his chest.

"Why me? You knew you had it, and yet you didn't even pause when I asked you to put a condom on."

"And for that, I'm sorry. I went in you raw for my own selfish reasons, and for that, I wish that I could turn back the hands of time."

Jade paused and thought about what she wanted to ask him. Her throat began to get that scratchy feeling that she always got right before she cried. *'Girl, you better the fuck not let not one tear fall from your eyes. He don't deserve to see you shed one motherfucking tear,'* she coached herself. She asked, "How did you get it?"

Jade heard Darion sigh. She knew that this was the last thing that he wanted to talk to her about, but she would feel better about knowing. Darion ran his fingers across his forehead as if he was contemplating on how he was going to answer. He figured he was already in a deep hole, so he might as well come on with the truth.

"I contracted the virus from my wife. Yajeel's mother was sleeping around on me. I worked so much that I never knew. I didn't even see any change in her activity. She worked in office buildings as a housekeeper, and that's where she was having an affair. I didn't find any of this out until she was on her death bed. She and a couple of coworkers were sleeping with several men in one of her main office buildings, until she met the man that gave her the virus. And this was six years before she confessed. She fell head over heels in love with him and even thought about leaving me and her son.

"When she began to get sick, she just thought that it was the flu. At this time, the affair that she was having with the dude began to dissipate. She thought he was trying to pull away from her. Gossip had begun to spread around the office that he had been out of work due to flu like symptoms. She managed to find out the hospital that he was staying in. I was at work when she took the day off and went to go visit him. Her coworker that gave her the info warned her not to go, but she went anyway.

"When she arrived, flowers in hand, she entered his room and noticed that he was in there alone. There were balloons and flowers surrounding the bed, but it was just him. She said that he looked pale and had open sores on his face and arms. His eyes were closed when she walked in, but he opened them when he felt her approach. My wife gave him the flowers and stared at him until he started to confess. He told her that he had been living with HIV for years, and was never on any meds. His HIV progressed to AIDS, and he was dying from that. He told her that she needed to get tested. They had unprotected sex several times, and it was a possibility that she had it. My wife was in denial when she found out that she had the virus. She told me that she didn't know how to tell me, and that she was ashamed. So instead of telling me, she continued to have unprotected sex with me. I didn't find out the truth until she got sick one day, and that shit took her from lying in bed to being admitted into the hospital. The look on her face when she told the doctor that she was HIV positive shook me to my core. The doctor had me tested immediately, and since I found out that I was HIV positive, I've been on my meds." Darion was happy that he had gotten that off of his chest.

A lone tear slid down Jade's face. She didn't realize she was holding her breath until she was gobbling up air like she had just been released from a death grip. She didn't know what to say. She wanted to feel bad for him, but how could she when he knowingly passed it to her?

"You sick son of a bitch. You passed that shit on to me. How dare you? Does Tanya have it? Does she know that you have it? I should beat you the fuck up in here," Jade yelled, going right back to livid. She jumped from the couch, causing Darion to do the same, just in case he had to defend himself.

"Tanya does know, and she does have it. She just doesn't didn't get it from me. She was born with it, and she takes her meds just like I do. That's why she is doing what she is doing. She knows that it will be hard to find a man that will fuck with her if they don't have it. I am sorry that I put you in this position."

Jade had been pacing the living room floor, wearing a hole

through her carpet, when she paused in mid-stride. She focused her attention on Darion. She stalked his way, with a mug on her face, and her finger pointed at him. She yelled, "Sorry is what you say when you cheat. Sorry is what you say when you step on someone's foot. Sorry is your mammy for giving birth to you. You don't say sorry when you give someone a death penalty. You could get your sorry ass out of my house. And let you or that funky bitch come back around here and see if I won't exercise the right to defend my home and blast y'all niggas back to whatever gutter y'all ratchet asses came from."

Darion was stuck in shock at how Jade was speaking. He didn't blame her for being mad, but he thought that if he was being honest, she would take it easy on him. He wasn't so sure now. Dropping the hammer and nails on her couch, Darion stumbled over his own feet as he quickly made it to Jade's front door.

"What about your window?" he managed to ask as he held the door halfway open.

Jade's eyes bulged out of her head as she grabbed the closest thing to her, which happened to be a vase filled with old flowers and water. Darion was out of the door before the vase crashed against the wall where he had just been standing.

"ARGGGGHHH," Jade screamed in agony. She pictured the conversation going differently in her head, which was the only reason as to why she even decided to have this talk with him. *'Why did I think that this shit was going to be a good idea?'* Jade thought as she swiped everything off of her coffee table. She should have just left well enough alone.

Jade caught herself getting ready to destroy her house, and she paused. With her right hand on her hip and her left hand on her head, she inhaled a few times, picked up her phone, and googled window replacement companies. Thankfully, they were able to send somebody out in an hour, and her windows would be fixed. Her next call was to reschedule with Sasha. She didn't have the mental capacity to deal with anything else.

Silencing her phone, Jade went to the kitchen and poured herself a glass of wine. Taking the bottle with her, she sat in her room until it was time for her to let the window people in.

Chapter Six

It was quitting time for Carmen, and her feet couldn't wait until she got home to soak. Her heels throbbed as she limped to her car. She got in her car, thinking about the trip to the grocery store that she had to make. Denise wanted to make her dinner, but she had to be the one to grab the items. She turned her radio up as she heard *Clout* by Cardi B and Offset. She danced in her seat as the beat drove her booty cheeks to pop one at a time. Her mood was instantly changed as she thought about the weekend approaching.

Turning into the parking lot for Price Chopper, she rushed to get out of the car and rushed inside to get the things she needed for dinner. She was in her own world in the seasoning aisle, trying to decide which brand of jerk seasoning she should get.

"This one right here, man. It's the right kind of spicy, and also, if you let it sit overnight, you will have seasoning straight down to the bone," a deep baritone voice said over her shoulder. She watched as a brown skinned, tattooed arm, reached over her shoulder, and grabbed one of the seasonings in front of her. The smell of his Dior cologne assaulted her nostrils.

"You think so?" she asked as she took the bottle from his hand. He was so close to her, she felt the heat from his body and quickly turned around, looking smack dead into his chest. Carmen was only five foot three inches, having to crane her neck to look up at him said that he had to be well over six feet.

"I know so. I use it all the time." He smiled. Bright white teeth almost knocked the wind out of her. She smiled herself. She didn't know how long it had been since a man had her smitten. This man had her smitten. Unconsciously, she bit her bottom lip as she looked up at him.

"What are you, a chef?" she asked.

His laughter thundered from his chest as he responded, "Actually, I am."

Carmen blushed as her smile brightened. She took a good look at this man and couldn't help but to notice how ugly-fine he was. He had the height that she liked in men, the dark skin that she liked, he was tatted, he had full lips, and a small nose. A few scars from acne adorned his face and she could get lost in his medium brown eyes.

"Oh," she responded. She didn't like the fact that she was voluntarily flirting with this man.

"If you don't mind me asking, do you plan on making jerk chicken tonight?" His eyes twinkled with humor as he tilted his head, looking at Camren's face lustfully.

Denise's face flashed to the forefront of her mind, and she shook off what she was feeling. It had been forever since she had that feeling when speaking with a man that she found attractive. Before Denise, Carmen was practicing celibacy, so this feeling that she was feeling for this man, was foreign, but felt good.

"Well, not me per se, but yes, that is the plan," she answered as she slid to the side to get from in front of him.

He picked it up and raised an eyebrow at her. Clearing his throat, he stepped back, giving her space. He responded, "That won't work. When making jerk chicken, you have to let that thing marinate over night. That's if you want to get all of the flavor."

"Thanks for the tip. I have to go," Carmen hurriedly replied. She grabbed the handlebar to her shopping cart and headed towards the end of the aisle.

"Wait," she heard him speak again, halting her in her steps. She turned to face him, and that damn smile. He continued, "You're beautiful. I was wondering if I could get your name and number. Maybe I can teach you a few tricks for cooking."

"Are you implying that I don't know how to cook?" Carmen asked, her hand on her hip, feeling offended.

"N-no. It was a corny attempt at a pickup line, which I now realize was horrible. I didn't mean to offend you."

Carmen eyed him. She said, "I was a little offended, but you're good."

He chuckled, "I'm a little rusty. It sounded good in my head."

"I can't give you my number. I'm with someone," she said, just barely above a whisper.

He heard her though and he nodded his head slightly as if to let her know that he understood. "A name wouldn't hurt though, right? Just in case I run into you, I can say hey."

"Carmen."

He reached his hand out to her as he said, "Bilal."

Hesitating, Carmen reached her hand towards him and took his hand into hers. They shook hands as they smiled at each other. Carmen let his hand go first, and soon as she did, she flew out of the aisle. She paid for her things, rushing to get home to Denise. She both liked and hated what she felt while talking to Bilal.

Carmen arrived home and took the bags inside of the house. Denise was in the kitchen playing soft jazz music while prepping onions and peppers. Carmen placed the bags onto the kitchen table and grabbed Denise by the waist.

"Well hello to you too, honey," Denise said. She used the hand towel to dry her hands as she wrapped her arms around the back of Carmen's neck and placed a kiss on her lips.

"I just missed you. That's all," Carmen replied as she pressed her body into Denise's, causing Denise's body to press against the counter. Carmen reached her hand to the back of Denise's neck and pulled her in for another kiss.

Things began to get heavy as Carmen reached under Denise's shirt and groped her titties. Denise let out a moan against Carmen's lips as she tilted her head back. Denise rubbed her hands up and down Carmen's back.

"Let me go take a quick shower. Forget dinner for right now," Carmen stated. She made eye contact with Denise and slowly walked away.

Denise didn't know what had gotten into Carmen, but she liked it. She did what her girlfriend asked her and left the kitchen. She heard the shower running as she made it to their room. Going inside of the closet, Denise looked for her gift bag she had hid a week ago, just for her to use for this night. Going into the bag, she pulled out a silk three piece set of lingerie. The shorts were emerald green with black lace trim, black lace thongs, and a black lace bralette. She grabbed her emerald green and black lace robe and laid it on the bed. Denise rushed to change into the lingerie. Putting her robe on, she tied the straps loosely around her waist and laid on the bed.

Soon after Denise was done changing, Carmen was coming into the bedroom in just a towel, her natural curly hair dripping wet. Carmen's eyes bulged at the sight of Denise. She had always seen her with barley enough clothes on, but the sight before her eyes had her pleasantly surprised. Her clit thumped as she used the towel to pat herself dry. Carmen made her way over to the bed and stood next to Denise. Softly, Carmen used her fingertips to run across Denise's soft skin. Denise looked at Carmen and smiled. No words needed to be exchanged in between the two.

Carmen climbed onto the bed, her feet resting on the sides of Denise's body. She bit her bottom lip as she lowered her body on top of Denise. Carmen never took charge, but meeting Bilal had her wanting to take charge. She used her index finger to grab at the lace on Denise's bra, exposing her chocolate colored nipples. Carmen leaned over and placed Denise's nipple into her mouth. Her tongue swirling around her nipple as her mouth suctioned her areola. Denise moaned and held the back of Carmen's head. Using her left hand, Carmen slid her hand down Denise's body and into her shorts. Carmen rubbed her fingers across Denise's wet clit in a circular motion.

"Mmm. Damn, babe," Denise moaned.

Carmen's response was to lick a trail from Denise's nipple, up to her neck, and trace her lips with her tongue. Carmen positioned her lips near Denise's ear and whispered, "You like that?"

Denise was on the verge of cumming all over Carmen's fingers as she shook while nodding her head. Carmen smiled against Denise's neck and dipped her fingers inside of her warm spot, while using her thumb to massage her clit. Soon after, Denise was moaning against Carmen's lips as her orgasm shook her body.

Carmen instructed Denise to lay directly in the middle of the bed on her back. Once Denise was comfortable, Carmen stood over her, with her legs straddling her body. She looked down on Denise, as she used her left hand to massage and twirl her nipple in between her fingers, and her right hand to slide her fingers between her wet slit.

"I don't know what has gotten into you, but I'm liking this," Denise remarked as her own fingers met her wetness.

Carmen wouldn't dare mention that she was visualizing the ugly-fine nigga she had met that day. With a smile on her face, Carmen slowly lowered herself over Denise face, her eyes rolling to the back of her head as Denise's tongue slid across her clit. Carmen rotated her hips as Denise held her up by placing her hands under her ass cheeks. Carmen took both of her titties into her hands and took turns between each one, flicking her tongue across her nipples.

"Ahh! Keep your tongue right there, baby," Carmen moaned out. Denise's tongue was applying the right amount of pressure to the bean of her clit and her legs shook as she was ready to release.

"You know what to do, baby. I've been waiting for this all day," Denise moaned into her pussy.

Carmen knew that Denise liked when she squirted on her. If they were in a different position, then she wouldn't mind. Carmen could squirt all over her face but she was scared that she would drown her.

"Ahh! Fuck! I'm coming, baby," Carmen yelled out, forgetting all about her concern of drowning Denise. *She a big girl, she can handle this. Oh my God,'* Carmen thought to herself. Her legs shook as she watched herself squirt all over Denise's face. When she was done, Carmen moved from over Denise and laid on the bed, her head slightly hanging off of the foot of the bed.

Denise used the sheet to wipe her face as she climbed on top of Carmen, not quite done with her yet. Her pussy was placed perfectly on her thigh, and she began to grind on her leg.

Carmen hated when she would squirt, she'd feel light-headed afterward. She tried not to do it often, but Denise knew what to do to make her cum that way. Denise had Carmen's nipple in her mouth and was moving her legs open. Denise moved them into the scissor position and got comfortable on her knees with Carmen's leg over her shoulder.

She massaged Carmen titty with one hand, and grabbed her ass cheek with the other. Denise moved in circular motions, her clit rubbing against Carmen's. Their moans were heavy, drowning out the macaroni being stirred in a pot sound that was caused by both of their pussies.

Carmen closed her eyes, visualizing Bilal on top of her instead of Denise. *'Oh this is not good,'* Carmen thought. She'd never fantasized about anyone since being with Denise. Visualizing was one thing, but thinking about a man had Carmen shook. She imagined Bilal on top of her, giving her death strokes. Her kitty was super wet.

"Hold on. Don't cum yet," Denise mentioned. She stopped grinding her pelvis into Carmen as she moved to the nightstand next to the bed. She reached into the drawer and pulled out a bullet the size of her pinky. With a smile on her face, Denise went back over to Carmen and placed the bullet between the two women's clits. She turned the bullet on to the medium setting. She continued to grind on Carmen as the bullet did its job. Both women were screaming out in ecstasy as it brought them to orgasm, causing the spot on the bed where they were to turn into a puddle. Legs shaking and not wanting to move another inch, they laid in the puddle, cuddled up in each other's arms.

"Mm. That was amazing. I don't even want to get up to cook," Denise said.

Stifling a yawn, Carmen responded, "You don't have to cook. We can order take out."

"But you like jerk chicken, and I wanted to cook it special for you tonight."

Carmen kissed Denise's arm, happy for her thoughtfulness. She said, "It's already getting late and I learned a new tip about jerk chicken today. You have to let the chicken marinate over night in order to get the seasoning in there good."

"Where did you hear that at?" Denise asked, looking down at Carmen.

"Just in passing at the grocery store. Let's just order take out and watch trashy shows in the living room," Carmen suggested. She was ready to do anything to take her mind off of Bilal.

Chapter Seven

The buzz of chatter surrounded Sasha as she sat at the bar inside of Wellington's, a restaurant located inside of the Renaissance Albany Hotel, on State Street, in Albany. She was done with court for the day, and a drink was well needed. After Sasha had won Nasir's case, it seemed like every criminal in the Capital District wanted to have her on their retainer. While it was a boost in her reputation, she could only take on the higher profiles. That meant more money in her pocket.

Sasha looked down at her phone and noticed that it was nearing eight o' clock at night. Mrs. Diane had texted her and told her that she would be keeping her girls for an extra two weeks. She was grateful for that. Outside of the circle that knew what was going on, Brandon's parents had no clue. Mrs. Diane said that since it was summertime and the kids were out of school, she was going to take her girls down to their beach house in Florida. She was grateful for that. She didn't know how her situation was going to play out, but she knew she had two weeks to figure it out.

Sasha wanted to be furious with Brandon, but she was no better. She was sleeping with Nasir every chance she got after he had revealed her husband's infidelities. In a way, she felt like she owed him. But that was only a small part. The bomb dick was just a bonus. Since her fight with Amekia, two weeks prior, she wasn't trying to take Nasir seriously. It seemed like the more they spent time with each other, the deeper her feelings got.

"Would you like another drink?" The bartender came over to Sasha while drying the inside of a glass. She looked down at her cup, which was damn near empty. The brown liquid was still cold, due to the ice that was slowly melting in her cup.

"Yes. But this time, bring me a double shot of peach whiskey," Sasha stated and threw the rest of her drink back.

"Bring her some water," a voice said from behind her.

She paused in her movements as she devoured his scent in deep breaths. She then turned on the bar stool and craned her neck to look up at the fine specimen that stood before her. A smirk displayed on her face as she said, "Don't listen to him. I need that drink, so if you want a tip, you will continue to bring me my drinks until I tell you to stop."

Nasir shot daggers at her. He knew that she was feeling a little tipsy by the way she spoke. There was a slight slur in her speech, and her words were aggressive. He asked, "How long have you been here?"

"Two hours. I got here after work," she answered. That much was pretty obvious. The maroon colored slacks that were fitted to her thick thighs and ass, and the gold colored blouse was a dead giveaway. Nasir took the seat next to her, while eyeing her. The bartender placed Sasha's drink in front of her and quickly walked away. He avoided the grill that rested on Nasir's face at all cost.

"Hard day at work?" Nasir asked.

Sasha cut her eyes at him but smirked as she noticed that his hair was freshly cut. He was rocking distressed blue jean shorts and a white, short sleeve Polo shirt. On his head sat a black and red fitted hat with the Yankee symbol on the front. On his feet were black and red Jordan 12's. He wore three thick ass diamond Cuban link chains around his neck that made noise every time he moved. On his left wrist was a white iced out diamond Miami Cuban link bracelet, and on his right wrist he rocked a gold Rolex Datejust 16233 watch with a red face, diamond's that replaced the numbers, and a diamond band. This man screamed money, and her panties screamed that she wanted him to touch her.

"Something like that. You look nice," Sasha complimented.

"Nice? Baby, I look the fuck good. You better know who you talking to out here, shorty," Nasir said, chuckling as he stood up and rocked side to side, showing off his look.

Sasha laughed, picked up one of his chains with her finger, and said, "Yeah, I see you looking like money."

"Damn right. I made it and I'm gonna for damn sure wear it. Thanks to my boo, I am now a free man, and free to bring out the pieces."

"If I would have known that you was holding like this, I would have charged you more than I did."

Nasir shook his head and looked seriously at Sasha. He said, "I'm serious though, Sasha. If it wasn't for you, I think that I would be still locked up. For what you did, I will be forever grateful to you."

Sasha twirled her wedding ring around her finger as she chugged her drink down. She asked, "Is that why you have been ignoring me?"

"What you talking about? You were the one who stopped answering me. Before winning my case, you ignored me because you found out what you found out about your husband."

"That I had no choice but to find out because you threw that shit all in my lap," Sasha announced, raising her voice. She continued, "If you wouldn't have done that, I still wouldn't have known. And you know what, I think I would have liked it that way."

Nasir was taken aback by her outburst. When he gave her the envelope, she was grateful. Now she wished she had never known. Looking around the restaurant, he noticed that people were beginning to stare. He leaned in real close to Sasha, causing her to lean back, almost leaning onto the patron behind her. He said, "Listen here, if you got some shit that you want to get off your chest, we can do so. But not in a room full of people. You know how fast these white people would call the police on us. One thing is for certain and two things for sure, shorty, I'm never seeing the inside of a jail cell again. Now get your blazer and your briefcase and lets fucking go before you have me out here looking like a nut ass nigga for going upside your head."

Sasha had never been spoken to like that before, not even by her husband. And while she didn't think that Nasir would go upside her head, she couldn't help but to be turned on by his aggressive tone. Sasha fumbled to grab her things as Nasir went into his pocket and threw money onto the counter. Sasha was surprised at the knot that he pulled out, and the bartender was even more impressed at the amount of money that was thrown on to the counter. He didn't make one noise as he grabbed the money up and cleaned up Sasha's mess.

Nasir walked in front of Sasha, head held high, smelling, and looking like a bag. Sasha followed behind him as he made a left to head to the elevators, instead of right to go outside. She didn't say a word, and neither did he. *Ding.* The elevator announced its arrival, and they entered. Still nothing was said. Nasir pressed the button for the ninth floor and watched their reflection in the doors. Once again, the elevator dinged and opened up. They exited, and Sasha followed Nasir. He placed the key card in the door and they walked inside.

"Put ya shit down and I'll fix us a drink," he said over his shoulder.

Sasha slowly made her way inside of the bedroom, taking in the beauty of the room. She often went to the hotel to visit the bar, and never had actually been inside of a room. The suite had a living room, kitchen, and bedroom with the view of the Albany night lights. She took her shoes off by the doorway, and placed her blazer and briefcase on the chair. She walked towards the window and looked out. *'Bitch you are married. Why do you feel the need to dig a bigger hole than you're already in?'* she scolded herself. She was lost in her thoughts and didn't realize that Nasir had crept up behind her. He was placing the drinks on the table, stalking her way.

"Look I," Sasha started but never got to finish.

Nasir placed his palms on the walls on either side of her head. He was close to her, so close she could hear his heart beating through his chest. Moving slowly, Nasir removed his hand from the wall and placed it on her neck.

Lightly squeezing, he moved in close to her and whispered, "Don't you ever in your life talk to me like that again. I had to put my gangsta on the back burner while I got this court shit situated, but make no mistake, shorty, you can't just talk to me any kind of way. You understand?"

"I got you. I just had one hell of a day and-"

"I don't care. When you see me and in my presence, whatever kind of day you had goes out the window. Apologize to Daddy." His warm tongue on her neck caused her to stammer her apology.

"S-s-sorry d-d-daddy," Sasha managed to say. She bit her bottom lip as she looked into Nasir's eyes. His hand was removed from her neck and busy trying to unbutton her pants.

"You should have done a better job at ignoring me. Cause I'm about to punish the shit out of you."

Sasha liked the sound of that. She wiggled her ass up out of her slacks as he popped her blouse, causing her buttons to fly all over the room. His lips instantly went to hers as he palmed her fat ass cheeks in his hands. This was the best part about fucking with Sasha for Nasir. He loved the thickness of her and wanted to experience this every day. Reaching to the back of her, he unsnapped her bra, allowing her titties to spill out. He hungrily took one of her breasts into his mouth and swirled his tongue around her nipple. Her eyes rolled to the back of her head. Nasir rubbed his hands all over her body as he felt his manhood getting hard. Sasha reached down and grabbed at his belt, helping him out of his pants, just like he had helped her out of hers.

Nasir walked Sasha to the bed and pushed her lightly onto the bed. He looked at her lustfully. Sasha pulled her panties down and rubbed her fingers over her clit. Nas wrapped his fingers around his dick and slowly stroked his dick. Nas' thoughts slipped back to the day that he killed his wife. The events moved fast in his thoughts. He had only been in jail for a year because he left the task of getting him a lawyer to some-one he trusted. People thought for sure that since he commit-ted murder, he was going to be locked down for a while. He thought so, too, until he had called his sister, Amekia.

Amekia and Nasir had never been that close because he left home at sixteen. She was only ten at the time and was heartbroken when he left. Nas left because he didn't agree with how his parents were living. He saw things that he didn't like, and when he decided to leave, he vowed that he would come back to get his sister. Time slipped from under him as he thrust himself in the drug game. He was making money hand over fist, and so his life of the past was no longer his concern.

When he got jammed up, the people he thought would have his back didn't, so he reached out to his sister. Thank God he always kept tabs on Amekia. He was grateful that she still had the phone number that she'd had for a few years.

He told her what happened with him. Before she agreed to help, she cursed him out something awful. She cried, telling him the awful things that she had to endure when he left. Thankfully, at the end of their conversation, she agreed to help him. She told him that she was best friends with a lawyer and she would see what she could do. He wasn't supposed to fall for Sasha, but he did. And here they were now, and Nasir was determined to make her his by all means.

"You want this dick?" Nasir asked, still stroking himself. Sasha was laying on her back, rubbing her clit in circular motions, and pinching her nipples.

"Please," Sasha moaned.

A smirk displaying on his face, Nas came completely out of his clothes, yanking Sasha to the edge of the bed. Tasting her was a must, and that was what he did. Her legs rested on his shoulders as he feasted on her. She tasted like peaches, and her nectar was coating his face. Nas got lost in her pussy as he swirled his tongue on her clit. Her moans invaded his ears as he switched from his tongue to his fingers. He spit on her pussy, giving it extra lubrication. He thrusted his fingers inside of her, as if he was serving her his dick.

Sasha was in ecstasy, as she laid there and came over and over again. Sex with her husband was okay at its best. He thought only of himself, and wanted to get it done and over with. Sex with Nasir was amazing. He took his time with her and made sure that she came several times, before he even stuck his dick inside of her.

Nasir flipped Sasha onto her stomach, as he stood there and took in the beauty of her booty. He knelt down on his knees, rubbed his hands on her cheeks, spreading them apart every time his hands moved up. Her sticky juices made noises. Nasir spread her cheeks apart and spit on her asshole right before he slid his tongue up and down her ass crack, dipping it in her ass every time he licked past the hole. Sasha was grasping at the sheets, trying to get away from the assault that he was giving her with his tongue.

"Ooh, I can't take no more," Sasha moaned, trying to flip over.

"Girl, if you don't stay your ass in that fucking position. Did I tell you to move?" Nasir growled under his breath.

Standing to his feet, Nasir pulled her by her hair to stand up with him. Her back was towards him and he wrapped his arm around her waist to get to her love box. She wasn't lying when she said she couldn't take it anymore. Her clit was sensitive, and she knew that mentioning it again would be pointless. His free hand wandered up her body and stopped at her neck, applying pressure. His dick was rock hard, pressing against her ass cheeks. Moving quickly, he pushed her into the doggy style position and entered her all at once.

"Shiiiit," they both hissed out because of how good each other felt. Nas made his dick jump inside of her before he began to slow stroke her.

"Nas, wait, we need a condom," Sasha moaned out. Although she was on a pill, she didn't know if he had dabbled in unprotected activity since the last time they had sex.

"Nah. This pussy is mine. I know for a fact you not giving it to homeboy, or anybody else."

"While that may be true, ssss, I don't know what you been doing since the last time we had sex."

"This your dick, baby. Ain't nobody else getting this shit," he grunted. And it was the truth. He may have been a kingpin, but he didn't make it a habit of going around giving his dick to just anybody, let alone doing it unprotected. He grabbed at her waist and rolled his hips as he picked up his speed.

Sasha took his word and threw her ass back. He was hitting spots that she didn't know she had. He placed his foot onto the bed so he could hit all of her walls. Her moans let him know that he was doing exactly that. She tried to keep up his pace, but he was drilling her like he was trying to reach her heart through her pussy. She was cumming again. With a smirk on his face, Nas pulled out of her, taking a look down at his dick. It shined with her juices as they dripped down onto the hotel carpeted floor. Sasha collapsed onto the bed with a smack to her ass.

"Move up some," Nas demanded.

This new Nasir that Sasha was experiencing was making her weak, and she didn't know if she liked it or not. The ball was just in her court, but now it seemed like Nas was the one leading. She did what he asked, soon feeling his weight on the bed. He kissed the back of her neck as he used his hand to raise one of legs higher than the other. He got comfortable on her back, causing her to hike her ass towards him. Yet again, he was entering her and putting his pipe game down. At this point, she was exhausted and ready to go to sleep, but she knew he hadn't cum yet. She was on orgasm number seven.

"Ooh, Nassss. This dick is so good," Sasha moaned.

"Oh, I know it is. Act right and you can get this dick all the time," he gloated. He knew what his sex game was like. Back before he got married, he used to have females going crazy over his dick. Coupled with his looks, he was the total package for a female. He liked the fact that Sasha was submissive to him. He was in control of that pussy, and he knew that in little time, she would be filing for a divorce against the fuck nigga she was married to.

"I'm cumming again," Sasha screamed out. This time she soaked the bed. He was rubbing her clit from behind while the tip of his dick was pounding away at her G-spot, causing her to squirt.

"I'm getting ready to cum, too. Come suck this dick," he, yet again, demanded. He was on his knees stroking his dick while Sasha was getting in a comfortable position to give him the best head she'd ever given him. Sasha licked the tip and sucked on the head before she swirled her tongue around the shaft, licking her juices off. She looked up at him as she opened her mouth and slid him inside. If she was a magician, she would have gotten a round of applause as she made his dick disappear down her throat.

"Oh, that's what you doing?" Nas said. He threw his head back at the feeling of her warm, tight, throat engulfing his dick. She was massaging his balls and humming on his dick, having his toes curl and his eyes roll to the back of his head. Nas grabbed her head and fucked her throat. He didn't care about the gag noises she was making. As long as she didn't throw up, they were cool. Nas was ready to come, and he pulled his dick out of her mouth.

"Say ahhh for Daddy," he growled, stroking his dick. Nas stood up while Sasha tucked her legs under her, sitting on her knees. He stroked himself he was letting his seeds go. Sasha's face was covered in his children and she didn't complain one bit. His nut was sliding down her forehead onto her lashes, dripping from her nose and onto her lips. Looking up at Nas, she licked her lips and winked at him.

He was now feeling lightheaded and needed to lay down. He had been holding that in since the last time they were together. Not even jerking off during the time they were apart was going to work for him. So he was backed up like a motherfucker, and was surprised that he didn't bust as soon as he entered her.

"Come lay with me, shorty," he said.

"Give me a second and let me wash my face." Sasha responded as she walked into the adjoining bathroom.

By the time she made it back to the bed, Nas was lightly snoring. Sasha had time to lay there and think about what it was that she was doing, and what it was that she wanted to do with her husband. Although she still loved her husband, she wasn't in love with him, and she thought that it was only right to serve him divorce papers. His and Amekia's betrayal was too unforgivable for her to say that she was going to stay and work on it. She refused to be the laughingstock.

***

Faint voices rang out in Sasha's head as she stirred in the bed. Rolling over to the side where Nas should have been, she kept rolling because his body wasn't there. Her eyes sprang open as she looked around the dark room. Her phone was on the nightstand, and she reached for it. It was going on two in the morning. The sound of a door closing caused Sasha to jump. With the sheet wrapped around her, she went to go look for Nas, hoping that it wasn't him leaving out of the door. She was surprised when she walked into the kitchen area and saw Nas putting food on plates and orange juice in glasses. She stood in the doorway and watched him.

"You gonna stand there or you gonna help a nigga out?" Nasir asked, never taking his eyes off of the task at hand.

"Nah, I think that you got it. I'll just sit here and look pretty," she chuckled, deciding to walk over to the table. Nas chuckled and continued to pile their plates with eggs, sausage, bacon, French toast, and waffles.

"Your stomach was growling in your sleep, hence the food. That motherfucker woke me up out my sleep."

"Stop bullshitting," Sasha laughed.

"I'm serious. That's the only reason why I'm up now. A nigga was sleeping good, too." He eyed her, causing her to blush. Nas sat next to Sasha, grabbing her leg, and putting it on his lap. He bit his bottom lip, not being able to advert his gaze. Sasha picked up her fork and began to eat, trying not to pay attention to his gaze. After a moment or two, Nas finally joined her.

"Nas, what is it that is going on between us?" Sasha asked

after they were done eating. They went back to the bed and decided on watching a movie until they fell asleep.

"What do you mean? You thought that I was just talking sex talk with you when I told you that this pussy is mine?" he responded while grabbing her pussy into his hand.

"No. I mean, yeah. I don't-"

"Shorty, you ain't gotta worry about nothing when it come to me. I mean what I say when I say it. You're mine. I know that you gotta get a divorce with this nigga, but I'll wait for you to take care of that, as long as I get to sleep and get up in this every night."

Sasha paused. While it sounded nice, that wasn't the reality of it. She knew Brandon, and she knew he would give her a hard time with the divorce. She said, "You know I'm the stupid one in all of this. After I got into a fight with Amekia, I had time to think back and try to see if there was any time that I missed any signs. And I did. Amekia, a couple of years ago, was going around talking about her new mystery man that she had. She said that she liked him but didn't know how promising their relationship would be. She claimed that he worked a lot, and she needed him to be able to make time for her. She wouldn't even show us a picture of him, but she did give us his name. She told us that his name was Donnie. I should have put two and two together, but Donnie is a common nickname. Everybody knew that Brandon's middle name starts with a D, but never knew what it was. He hates his middle name because it's a nickname, instead of a name. Out of the circle, I was the only one who knew his middle name, of course.

"One day we were all hanging out, not a regular girl's night, just friends getting together. Brandon and Amekia were in the kitchen with two other friends, but they were having their own conversation. I was rushing into the kitchen to get another bottle of wine and I heard her say Donnie. I stumbled in my walk, but then disregarded it as having too much wine. I should have known better."

Nasir listened to her intently. He hated that it was his sister involved, and he knew that if that got out, his chances with Sasha were going to go right out of the window. By all means, he was going to keep that part of his life a secret.

"Don't worry about it, babe. If you allow me, I will help you move past that. You are a beautiful woman, inside and out, and you don't deserve what happened to you. Let's get some rest. I got a long day ahead of me," Nas spoke, changing the subject. He rolled them over into the spooning position, wondering if his secret came out, how he would fix the trouble that could arrive.

Mimi

Chapter Eight

It had been a month since Amekia gave birth to her daughter, and she couldn't wait for the doctor to give her the clear to go back to work. She loved being at home with her daughter, but she was starting to lose her mind. If she didn't have to go out, she stayed home. The July heat was disrespectful in 2019, and she didn't want to subject her baby to that.

In just three days, she was due to go to court with Sasha and Brandon, and she was sick with worry. Sasha had an upper hand on her because she knew the law. But one thing was for certain, Amekia knew that there was no way there would be a judge that would award Sasha custody unless she was abusing or neglecting her child. Amekia knew that she was just trying to get some get back, but it still didn't stop her from worrying.

Brandon had stepped up and was seeing Aziyah more often. Most times, he would come straight from work to come see her, and other days he would come when he had a spare day off and spend hours with her. Amekia enjoyed their bonding and never put up a fuss when he stopped by. She knew that with what he had going on at home, his two other daughters, and work, he was doing the best that he could, and that was all that she could hope for.

It was a Thursday evening that Amekia was enjoying by herself. Carmen's mother offered to watch Aziyah so Amekia could have time to herself. Amekia put up a fight. She didn't feel right pawning her daughter off to Carmen's mother. Ms. Boward called Amekia herself and cussed her out. She told her that when someone is offering the help, to take it. She told her how hard it was when she had Carmen and Ashlyn and nobody in her family wanted to help. She told Amekia never to be ashamed or feel like less of a mother to Aziyah if she took a break. More babies in this new age were dying due to the mothers killing them or hurting them because they took too much on at once. Once Amekia saw it the way Ms. Boward had put it, she packed her daughter an overnight bag and took her over.

She had just settled onto the couch, about to hit play to catch up on her show, *Claws,* when her doorbell rang. She put her glass of wine on the coffee table and strutted to her door. She was surprised to see Jade and Carmen on the other side of the door.

"What the fuck y'all doing here?" she asked.

"We couldn't let you spend the night alone while Aziyah was away," Jade commented. She raised a bottle of wine up and strutted inside. Carmen had bags of food from a Chinese takeout spot down the block.

"I would have preferred to spend it alone." Amekia playfully rolled her eyes and closed the door behind them.

The three friends sauntered into the living room after they had gathered two more glasses from the dining room. Instead of watching *Claws,* they decided to catch each other up with what they have been up to.

Amekia was up first. She told her friends all about how Brandon had really stepped up and started seeing Aziyah more often. She let them know that she wasn't aware if Sasha knew or not, but even if she did, she had no place to voice her opinion. Sasha had nothing to do with her baby, and it was going to stay that way until she could come to grips that her husband had an outside child.

"I'm still in disbelief that you and Brandon had a baby together. We thought you hated his guts this whole time," Carmen retorted.

"Most times, it was because I did hate his guts. He would intentionally make snide remarks when he would overhear us talking and I would bring up an old fling. That shit used to burn him up. But like I told him, he had no room to feel a certain way. He had a wife, and I was free to do whatever it was my heart desired, even though I didn't. My dumb ass stayed faithful to him while he went home to Sasha every night."

Jade asked, "Did you ever want him to leave Sasha?"

Amekia pondered that question. She did want him to leave her, but not for him to be with her. Choosing her words wisely, Amekia responded, "Yes. Only because he was so unhappy. Let me make this clear, though. Not so that he could be with me. Brandon and I had something more than just sex. We were really best friends, and whenever he would feel like he wasn't happy, he would discuss his feelings with me. He told me that Sasha had changed. He knew that sex wasn't a big thing in a marriage, but it was one thing that he mentioned that she withheld. She would be too tired, or just didn't want to. And when they did have sex, she would just worry about getting her rocks off, instead of making sure both of them got off.

"It was so depressing to hear the stories that he would tell me. So I gave him a solution. Leave her. He said that he could never do that to his kids. So he just continued to have me on the side."

For Carmen and Jade, that was a lot to process. They didn't judge Amekia for what she did, but to some extent, they understood. They both had voluntarily and involuntarily been a man's side piece. But never did it ever get that deep for them. So they got it, but never would they do it to a friend. That's just one line that they couldn't see themselves crossing.

"That was deep, Amekia. And you know we are always going to have your back. But Sasha's, too," Carmen responded, while rubbing her hand across the top of Amekia's.

"I never want y'all to choose sides, so of course, I understand that. This whole situation is messed up. While I want to apologize profusely to Sasha and let her know how sorry I am, I just can't bring myself to do it. Not because I know what I did was the most ultimate, unforgivable, betrayal, but because she bucked at me first, and going around telling people that I swung first."

Jade and Carmen's mouth dropped open at what Amekia had just revealed. Jade said, "I know you fucking lying. Who the fuck she told that?"

"Her husband," Amekia answered with the roll of her eyes.

"I can't believe she said that."

"Believe it, honey. Anyway, my mess is exhausting, what y'all heffas been up to? Anything juicy going on with y'all?"

Carmen and Jade looked at each other, and then at Amekia. Jade wasn't telling them jack shit, until she was ready to tell them. Carmen decided that Jade was taking too long, so she opened her mouth. She didn't want to say what she had being dealing with internally, but she couldn't talk about it with Denise. She knew she could count on her girls not to say anything to Denise. After all, they were her friends first, and that had to count for something.

"Well, a little over a month ago, I met someone in the grocery store," she said embarrassingly. She sank into the back of the couch, wishing that it would swallow her up.

"What?" Both Jade and Amekia stated in shocked unison.

"Denise wanted me to pick up some items one night so that she could make jerk chicken. That whole week she heard me saying that I wanted jerk chicken, and she thought it would be a cute idea to make me dinner when I got off work. While I was looking at the different kinds of jerk seasoning, there was someone watching me, and told me which one was the best. Gave me a tip about how if you let it sit overnight, the flavor would be all up and through the chicken. He wanted my number, but I told him that I had someone and just gave him my name. He said it would be just in case he saw me again and he could say hi."

"He?" Again they said in unison.

"Well, I'll be damned. This is juicy," Jade remarked as she took a sip from her wine glass.

"Yes, he. And, y'all, he was fine. Like you know the kind of fine where he ugly, but still something about him his fine."

"Ugly fine. That's how I like them," Amekia stated, sipping from her glass as well.

"Ever since I saw him, I've been thinking about that motherfucker, like borderline obsessing over him. I don't even know him, and I'm lusting about seeing him again. It's gotten so bad that I sometimes fantasize about him while me and Denise are getting down and dirty. I feel so bad."

"Chile, the teas," Jade murmured loud enough for them to hear. Both Carmen and Amekia laughed.

"It's okay, honey. You are a woman, who has had sexual relations with a man, so it's natural for you to feel that way towards a man. Quiet as it's kept, I think these lesbian women be fantasizing about these men, too. Women are naturally attracted to men, whether they full on dyking or not," Jade responded.

"Jade. Girl, you ain't never gonna have any filter on your mouth, will you?" Amekia asked.

"Hell no. I was like this when y'all met me, and y'all hoes gonna keep getting this," Jade responded, causing Carmen and Amekia to bust out in laughter.

"What do I do?" Carmen asked, getting serious.

Amekia thought about her answer before she spoke. She wasn't in the business of telling anybody what to do, but her friend was looking for advice. She said, "Your best bet is just to leave it alone. There are over sixty thousand people living in Schenectady. Do you know how likely it would be for you to run into him again? Focus on your relationship with Denise."

Carmen knew Amekia was right. She had a good thing going with Denise, and she for damn sure didn't want to fuck it up. Carmen was confused with how they decided to fuck with each other, and it had been forever since she was loved on by another person. She never thought that it would be with a woman. She was deep in her thoughts when she caught the end of what Jade was saying. She thought she heard her wrong, so she shook her thoughts and asked Jade to repeat herself.

Jade stared at the wall that was in front of her, trying to avoid eye contact with her friends. The tears welled in her eyes but didn't drop. She said, "I am HIV positive."

Carmen and Amekia gasped at what she said. They looked at each other for a quick second, and then both women thrusted themselves at Jade, embracing her in a hug. As soon as they embraced her, the tears poured from her eyes. She felt foolish because all she had done was cry since finding out her diagnosis. With everything in her, she wanted the tears to stop, but knowing that she had shorter time to be on this earth hurt her soul.

"Oh, babe. Stop crying," Carmen croaked, holding back her own tears. She rubbed Jade's back as she tapped at the tears in the corners of her eyes.

"I can't stop. Ever since I found out, I have been crying. I just want this to end, and I even contemplated doing so, too. But once I found out that Amekia named me Aziyah's Godmother, I knew I couldn't just think about the death sentence that I got. I knew that I had to start living. If something was to happen to Amekia, Aziyah is my responsibility. I just want the tears to stop. I am not a weak bitch."

Amekia said, "We know you not weak. Maybe the crying is good for your soul. Maybe one day you will wake up and stop crying and the inner bad bitch will come out and give you a new outlook on life. There is nothing that you can do differently except take your meds and take one day at a time. It's going to take time, but you will get there, babe. Now let's dry your eyes and enjoy this night, while I don't have my baby."

Laughter erupted, but soon was cut short when there was knocking on the door. Whoever it was came over with a point to prove because there was no way in hell somebody she knew was knocking instead of using the bell. The girls got up from the couch and made their way to the door. Amekia looked through the glass door panel and instantly grew angry. She swung the door open, causing Sasha to jump back.

"What the fuck are you doing here?" Amekia asked through gritted teeth.

Sasha looked between the girls that she used to call her best friends. She still considered Jade and Carmen her friends, but the way that things had been going, she knew before long she wouldn't even be speaking to them. Sasha said, "Can we talk? Privately?"

"Fuck no! You lucky I don't beat your ass." Amekia was too through, and she wanted to beat the fuck out of Sasha.

Sasha shuffled from one foot to the next. She rolled her eyes and said, "Look, I just came by to tell you that I dropped the custody hearing. You should be receiving a letter in the mail by next week."

"What?" Amekia asked astonished.

Carmen was infuriated. She wanted to know why she would put Amekia through the worry of losing her child if she was only going to drop the case.

Amekia asked, "So you just basically did that for a show? Tell me why I shouldn't beat your ass right now."

"What made you change your mind?" Jade asked. She asked the question that both Carmen and Amekia wanted to know, but were too mad to ask.

"I'm filing for a divorce," Sasha stated, and sucked up tears that were threatening to spill over.

Amekia stepped closer to Sasha and said, "You didn't drop the case because you're filing for a divorce, you dropped the case because you don't have probable cause to even seek custody. Aziyah isn't being abused or neglected, and you didn't want to appear in front of a judge, looking like the scorned wife. Fuck you, Sasha. If the shoe was on the other foot, and it was you who would have slept with my husband and had a child with him, I wouldn't even had played with you like that."

"If the shoe was on the other foot, I wouldn't have slept with your husband. Cause see, that's the difference between a little girl and a grown ass woman. While you out here trying to carry yourself like a woman, you are in fact a little girl, sleeping with men that ain't yours because of daddy issues. You looking for love in all the wrong places and, baby girl, if you think you found that in my husband, you are sadly mistaken," Sasha replied with a smirk on her face.

She hadn't gone there to read Amekia for filth, but Amekia had a slick ass mouth, and sometimes you had to fight fire with fire. For once, she was glad somebody put Amekia in her place, even gladder that it was her. She had it coming. With satisfaction, Sasha turned her back and began to descend down the porch stairs. Sasha was almost to the last step when she felt an excruciating pain sear through her scalp as she tumbled to the ground, hitting her back against the concrete steps. Amekia was on top of her before she realized what was going on.

"I'm done playing with your ass," Amekia yelled as Sasha kicked and screamed.

"Get this bitch off of me," Sasha yelled, wishing that Jade or Carmen would hurry up and come to her rescue.

What she didn't realize was that they were trying to pull Amekia off, but when angry, Amekia had the strength of an ox, and it was no easy feat for them to do. Amekia stumbled over Sasha's feet and that gave her leverage. She pushed off of Amekia and got on top of her, molly wopping her in the face. Constant blows were delivered to Amekia's face. Sasha was getting her back for last time.

Finally, Carmen and Jade grabbed Sasha off of Amekia. Instantly, Amekia got up from the ground and tried to get at Sasha, but was stopped when she felt arms around her waist. She didn't know who it was and started swinging. Carmen and Jade were still holding Sasha, and her instinct was to fight the person off.

"Yo, Amekia. Chill man." It was Brandon. He was busy trying to dodge her blows when he felt blows to his back. It was Sasha. He turned around to try and stop Sasha from hitting him when Amekia came around him and dragged Sasha to the ground by her hair.

"Bitch-bitch-bitch," Amekia yelled as she beat her fists into Sasha's back.

Carmen and Jade were through with the scene that was unfolding in front of them. Before they managed to move again, Amekia stopped fighting Sasha and went to sit on her stairs, out of breath. Her shirt was torn, there was a knot on her forehead, blood was pouring from a split lip, and her hair was all over her head. Brandon helped Sasha up off the ground. She looked even worse than Amekia did. The knots on Sasha's head were meme worthy. She was completely out of her shirt and bra. Her left eye was swollen shut, the right one was on its way, there was a trail of blood from her ear down her cheek, and her bottom lip was swollen twice its normal size.

"Is y'all finished or is y'all done? 'Cause this is ridiculous. Y'all too motherfucking grown to be out here in the fucking street fighting like dogs, like y'all wasn't just friends," Jade yelled. She'd had enough. There was a possibility that she could leave this earth before they did and this wasn't how she wanted them to be when that time came.

"Jade she attacked me first. You saw it with your own damn eyes," Sasha yelled trying to smooth her hair out. Brandon was trying to help her by giving her the pieces of her shirt from off of the floor, but she snatched away from him.

"You damn right, I did. You out here lying saying I attacked you the first time. Now you can really tell people that I did," Amekia yelled, anger dripping from her voice.

"Look, if y'all gonna fight every time y'all see each other, then y'all need not to. At this point, it's becoming too redundant. If y'all not gonna hash out y'all problems, then stay fifty feet apart," Carmen stated. She was over the scene. She knew the cops were soon going to be coming, and she didn't want no parts.

"What the hell are you doing here?" Sasha asked looking Brandon up and down.

"I came to -" Brandon started, but was cut off by Amekia. She was now standing in front of the stairs with her hands on her hips and a smirk on her face.

"He came to see his daughter," Amekia sneered.

"Amekia, I could have told her that. And if you didn't cut me off, I was getting ready to," Brandon stated. He didn't need her to speak for him, and he knew he was soon going to get irritated.

"How long has this been going on?" Sasha asked. She was hurt, but didn't expect less from Brandon. The daughters that she shared with him were well taken care of. He may have said that he would have given up his rights but she knew that he wouldn't follow through with it. It was just talk because he was a great father.

"For a month, Sasha. I would have told you, but I don't even see you no more. I've been trying to talk to you to make things right," Brandon expressed, damn near sounding like he was about to break down crying.

Amekia rolled her eyes at the display and then decided to go back in the house. Jade and Carmen followed, and soon Sasha walked away leaving Brandon there looking stupid.

Mimi

Chapter Nine

August 2019

A bad thunderstorm was brewing for the Capital District, and people were preparing as if it was a hurricane coming. Carmen was excited to be heading home from work. Denise had started a new job at Albany Medical Center, working in the emergency room. Denise had been trying to secure a spot there for years, while working at little odd jobs. She got in after the second fight between Sasha and Amekia. This was the first night they were going to be home at somewhat the same time, and they couldn't wait.

Thankfully, Denise was off two hours before the storm was supposed to hit. She rushed out of the hospital like her life depended on it. The wind was crazy, almost knocking her over as she tried to make her way to her car. Turning the key in the ignition, Denise picked up her phone to send a text to Carmen, letting her know that she was on her way home and that dinner would be done by the time she got home. When she was done, she put the car in drive, drove to the nearest gas station, and filled up her tank.

"Miss, do you need any help?" a baritone voice spoke, startling Denise.

"Ooh shit! You scared the mess out of me," he stated, as she grabbed at her chest. Lightly chuckling to herself, she shook her head no to answer the man's question.

"I'm sorry for scaring you. I only asked because you looked distracted."

"Oh. I'm just ready to get home. This storm is supposed to be really bad, and I don't want to be caught in it."

"I don't blame you," he chuckled. Denise was placing the gas nozzle back in its place when she turned and looked at the man that spoke to her. Yes, she was a lesbian and attracted to women, but this man, this man that stood before her was the epitome of a black God. He was super tall, cut up, and had a smile that made her panties moist. She caught herself staring at him when he looked at her with question in his eyes.

"Thank you for offering your assistance," Denise said politely, as she went to open her door.

He licked his lips smoothly, like LL Cool J, and looked at her. His eyes penetrated her, and she could have sworn he had just took her soul. He said, "My name is Trey, and yours beautiful?"

"D-Denise," she stuttered. *'Girl, get yourself together. Fuck wrong with you,'* she thought to herself.

"It's nice to meet you, Denise. You got a man?"

"No. I got a girl."

Trey chuckled, and said, "Damn."

"What?" she asked. Denise was curious as to why he had the response that he had.

"It's nothing to worry your pretty little head about."

In that moment, Denise got a text from Carmen, letting her know that she would be a little late. She responded with a frown on her face, and placed her phone back in her pocket. Looking up at Trey, she said with a smile, "It was nice meeting you. I gotta go."

***

Carmen stood in the lobby of her job and looked out at the pouring rain. It was so bad that she was barely able to see in front of her. She wondered how she was going to get home. Thunder boomed loudly, causing Carmen to move away from the door. Just that fast, the thunder came and the rain slowed down just enough for Carmen to run to her car.

"Lord, please let me make it home," Carmen silently prayed. Backing out of her parking space, she carefully drove home. The rain, once again, picked up, and Carmen found herself praying frequently throughout her journey home. All she needed was to get into an accident. The ride that would usually take her twenty minutes to get home, took forty, due to the weather. As she parked in front of her house, she sighed, grateful that she made it home in one piece. Grabbing her purse from the passenger seat, she rushed to get out of the car and to her door, getting soaked on the way.

Entering her home, she took her shoes off at the door. She wondered where Denise was at. Her car was in front, so she knew she had made it home. Carmen wanted nothing more than to fall into her arms after the day she'd had. She had a patient in with her son, who had to be around ten. The parent was clearly on some type of drugs, and the child had many bruises across his back and legs. CPS was called, and it pained Carmen that the boy was sadder that he was being torn away from his parental unit, than he was of the bruises that the doctor found.

Carmen made her way to the bedroom she shared with Denise, but was met with an empty room. Camren's eyebrow raised in confusion. *'Where the fuck could she be?'* Carmen thought. For the hell of it, she checked the bathroom and met with the same thing that she did with their bedroom. Carmen had a spare bedroom, but didn't understand why Denise would go there. Carmen paused in her steps before she headed to the room. *'Maybe she went to the corner store and that's why her car is still there,'* Carmen thought to herself. She was about to turn around and head back to her bedroom to get out of her wet clothes, but something dropped, and she stopped moving.

Carmen walked toward where she thought the sound had come from, and coincidentally, it was the spare bedroom.

Reaching for the doorknob, she thought she should have grabbed a knife from the kitchen in case there was a robber in her house. Opening the door and rushing in to scare the robber, Carmen was stopped in her tracks, and her breath was stuck in her chest.

There, in front of her, was her girlfriend, the woman who she loved and thought several times that she was worthy of her proposing to, in a compromising position. The tears welled in Carmen's eyes as she tried to make sense of what was in front of her. Denise was lying on her back, one leg in the air, the other stretched across the bed, and a fine ass chocolate male between her legs.

"Baby," Denise shouted, causing dude to pause mid-stroke. He looked at Denise in confusion, and realized that she was staring in Carmen's direction. He moved from between Denise's legs, and tried to cover himself with the sheet. Denise threw her hands over her face in embarrassment.

"Bilal?" Carmen asked in shocked. The man that she had been lusting over was there in her house, fucking on her girlfriend, no less.

"Umm. Hey?" he asked, not knowing what to say. What kind of luck did he have that the chick that he met at the gas station was the girlfriend of the chick that he couldn't stop thinking about from the supermarket?

"Trey, how do you know my girlfriend?" Denise asked side-eyeing both of them. Denise wondered if there was a possibility that this man had done the same thing he had done with her, to Carmen.

"Trey? He told me his name was Bilal," Carmen said breathlessly.

"I think it may be time for me to go," Bilal said, while getting up from the bed.

"Nah, nah, nigga. I think you need to stay 'cause both of

y'all got some explaining to do," Carmen stated. Her initial shock of hurt wore off, and she was straight up pissed off.

"Baby, I'm so sorry. I didn't mean for this shit to happen. I can't even lie and say it's not what you think, you witnessing this shit with your own eyes. I can only apologize," Denise stated, as she tried to hold back her tears. Denise knew that she went overboard. Denise knew that she was about to lose Carmen. She had been the best thing that had happened to her, and she managed to fuck it up.

"All this time, I thought you was *'team lesbian'* and you out here sneak dicking? And I thought I was a bad person for lusting after this man day in and out," Carmen responded, while looking over at Bilal as he sat there with a smirk on his face. Carmen folded her arms across her chest and continued, "I don't know what you sitting there smirking for? What the fuck is so amusing to you?"

Bilal looked between Carmen and Denise and couldn't help that his mind easily slipped into the gutter. He thought about the many different positions that he would have both of them in. A smile appeared on his face. He had never been in a situation like this, and his mind was taking him elsewhere. Finally, he decided to use his deep voice and said, "I don't know what you want me to say, pretty lady. But I will give y'all some time and leave up out of here."

"Yeah, you do that. Take this bitch with you," Carmen stated, and turned her back to walk out of the room.

Denise's mouth hung open as she jumped out of the bed, wrapping the sheet around her body.

"Carmen! Please don't do this. I'm sorry," Denise whined after Carmen.

Carmen kept her mouth shut as she went inside of their bedroom and began searching through the closet. Denise stood by the door, now in full blown tears, begging Carmen to just hear her out. Carmen found what she was looking for and swung around towards Denise. Denise instantly stopped blabbering as she stared down the barrel of Carmen's gun.

"When you pulled me from off of the bridge, I vowed to myself and God that if you stayed in my life, I would make sure that I would never do anything to hurt you, to never put you in the position to have to save me from a moment like that ever again. I would never imagine that you would stoop so low as to fuck a random nigga. Oh no, but you just had to take it further and do it in my house, the house that I've opened up to you for several months now. How dare you betray me like that," Carmen said. Her voice shook, but her aim was steady.

Bilal came inside of the room, and Carmen's aim went to him, causing him to pause in his footsteps and hold his hands up. He said, "Whoa, pretty lady. I was only coming to let y'all know that I was up out of here. Also, to apologize on my behalf for the fucked-up situation. Shorty told me she had a girl, and I was gonna leave it be, but shorty asked me to follow her here."

Denise couldn't believe what he'd just said. Granted, it did happen that way, but she had already done enough damage, she didn't want to add that bit of news on Carmen. Denise wanted to protest when she noticed Carmen look in her direction with hurt all over her face.

"You call yourself a man, but you spilling all the beans on how it went down. If you don't want a hot one in your ass, then you better take your ass on, 'cause I'm 'bout two seconds from pulling this trigger," Carmen stated coolly. She was hurting so bad inside, and she didn't know how long she was going to be able to keep up the façade. Carmen didn't have to tell Bilal twice, as he turned and hightailed it out of the house.

"Carmen," Denise sighed.

"I'm not telling you again to get the fuck out. When you

decide to come get your shit, make sure you have a police escort with you 'cause there ain't no telling what I'm gonna do if you show up here by yourself."

Denise knew that this was a fight that she wasn't going to win. Instead of staying and possibly fucking up the situation even worse, she decided to gather her clothes from the guest bedroom and leave while Carmen still had some sense in her to not pull the trigger.

Hearing the house door slam shut for the second time, Carmen lowered her arm, placing the gun on the dresser, and took a seat on the bed. The tears immediately fell, causing Carmen to let out a blood curdling scream. This hurt was hitting different, as she sat on the edge of the bed and cried. It felt like her heart was taken from her chest and broken into a million pieces. *'God what did I do to deserve this?'* She questioned. She knew that things were too good to be true between her and Denise, but damn, why did it have to happen this way?

Carmen's phone rang in her purse. She wanted to ignore it, but the gospel music that played through the speaker, told her that it was her mother calling her. She grabbed the phone, and slid her finger across the screen, answering without saying a word.

"Carmen, baby?" Carmen's mother asked through the phone. All day, Ms. Broward had a bad feeling in the pit of her stomach. There was something telling her to call her children to make sure that they were okay. She'd already spoke to Ashlyn, and it was Carmen's turn.

"Ma-ma-mama," Carmen stuttered out as the tears fell from her eyes.

"Oh, baby. What's wrong?"

"She cheated on me, mama," Carmen managed to say. She was still in disbelief as she let those words slip from her lips.

"What?" Ms. Broward yelped through the phone. Ms.

Broward grew up in the times where dating the same sex was seen as a sin, but when her daughter told her that she was with a woman, she let what she knew from growing up to slide. Ms. Broward had her reservations, but in the day and age that they were living in, she went with the flow and accepted it. Ms. Broward wasn't and wouldn't ever be in a position to judge anyone and who they loved. The sins of one person were left up to God and God only.

"I walked in on her cheating on me."

"And she did it in your house?" Ms. Broward was fuming. In her eyes, cheating was wrong, but doing it in the same household that you shared with your spouse was the ultimate disrespect.

"Mama. This hurts so bad. I don't know what I did to deserve this."

Ms. Broward felt bad for her daughter. Shaking her head on the other end of the phone, Ms. Broward said, "Baby, God got a funny way of showing you people's true colors. She may have been good for you in that moment, but God was preparing you for something major. The devil wears plain clothes, too, baby. Always remember that. Something drastic was going to happen, and God put a little stop in that. Thank him that he showed you what she is really about before you were dragged through mud."

"You know what the crazy part is, mama? The man she was cheating on me with, I had met a few weeks ago at the supermarket. I was lusting over that man every day, only for me to come home and see he had gotten between my girl-friends legs instead."

Ms. Broward gasped, taking a second to get her thoughts together. When she was sure that she was able to speak, Ms. Broward said, "She cheated on you with a man? I thought that she only liked women?"

"I thought the same thing, too, mama."

"Lord, forgive me, but what are these women out here doing? They out her sneak dicking, just wanting to pass diseases around."

Carmen erupted in laughter. She was truly her mother's child when it came to saying things that were on her mind. Wiping the tears from her eyes, Carmen said, "Thank you, Mama. I really needed that laugh. That was my same response when I caught her in the act."

Speaking with her mother made Carmen feel a little better about the situation. Maybe God was trying to show her something, and it just so happened that he showed her in one of the worst ways ever. By the time she had gotten off of the phone with her mother, the rain had stopped, and the sun was even trying to make an appearance. Carmen got out of her wet clothes and began to gather Denise's things for her to grab at a later date. She was done.

Mimi

Chapter Ten

"Mama," Alexis and Aliana yelled as they jumped from the back seat of their grandparents' all black Yukon. Sasha stood on her porch with a smile on her face. She missed her girls, and was grateful to her in-laws for stepping in while she silently battled a hint of depression. Her girls were on their way to Florida when her mother-in-law decided to stop by. As her girls neared, she bent down to receive them in open arms.

"Hi, my babies," Sasha expressed, once they were in her arms. Looking beyond them, she noticed that her mother-in-law had gotten out of the truck with a scowl on her face. *'Fuck wrong with her?'* Sasha thought. Betty folded her arms across her chest and made her way over to Sasha, watching the interaction, waiting for her granddaughters to run in the house so she could speak with Sasha alone.

"Mama, guess where we going?" Alexis asked.

"Let me see. I think I heard that you girls were going to visit a farm," Sasha said, while holding her index finger against her chin.

The girls giggled and replied, "No."

"Why don't you tell me then?"

"Mama, you got to guess." Aliana smiled a toothless smile.

Sasha did the same motion with her finger on her chin, appearing as if she was in deep thought. Snapping her finger as if she'd had an epiphany, Sasha responded, "Grammy is taking y'all to the McDonald's y'all like, the one with the playground inside."

The girls fell out laughing at how silly their mother was being. Both of the girls shook their heads and said, "No! She's taking us to Florida."

"Oh wow! You girls are about to go all the way to Florida

without your mama?"

"Yes," Alexis stated.

"Alexis wants to go see alligators, but Pawpaw said that it's too dangerous," Aliana expressed.

"That's because it is. Grammy and Pawpaw have to protect you guys while y'all away. So no alligators this time, Alexis."

"Aww man," Alexis moaned.

Betty cleared her throat, and said, "Girls, go ahead inside to go get your bears so that we can go catch our plane."

"Yes, ma'am," they said in unison, and ran passed Sasha.

Sasha exhaled as she took a seat on the stairs. Betty was still standing with her arms folded, while watching Sasha. A moment or two passed before either one said anything.

It was Betty that broke the ice. She said, "A divorce is not an option in this family."

Sasha slanted her head to look at Betty, raising her hand just above her eyebrows to shield the sun rays that were beating on her face. She cleared her throat, and asked, "Excuse me?"

"Brandon has been stopping by the house more than usual, lately, and I noticed. His father hasn't, so I brought it up to him. I asked him why he was around so often. He told me that he did the most unforgivable thing to you, and now you are talking about seeking a divorce. Whatever it is that he did, forgive him. As I have stated, divorce isn't an option."

Sasha chuckled, and she tried to wrap her mind around what Betty had just said. She couldn't believe that this old bat was suggesting such a thing. Sasha's relationship with Betty was a rocky one. Sometimes, they liked each other, other times, they were willing to rip each other's heads off. In this instance, it was the latter. It took Sasha a few moments to respond. She knew that if she didn't, there was going to be words exchanged and the girls wouldn't make it to Florida. She was petty like that, and the girls were already excited. Sasha didn't want to take that from them.

"So you telling me to forgive your son, who slept with, and had a baby with my best friend? Chile, bye," Sasha rebutted.

"Men do shit like that all the time, Sasha. No one is perfect. You don't think marriages go through things? How do you think Robert and I have lasted so long? Men are going to cheat, no matter what, and it's something that women have to endure."

"We don't live in those times no more, Betty. Whether you or your son like it or not, I'm filing for a divorce. And not even you can talk me out of it."

Betty sighed, and asked, "I wonder what your mother would think of this? God rest her soul."

Sasha's chest tightened at the fact that Betty brought her mother up. Betty and her mom had been friends for years. That's how Sasha and Brandon had gotten together in the first place. Sasha stood to her feet, and retorted, "Don't you dare bring my mother into this. She isn't here to defend anything that you say about how she may feel. And truth be told, she would have been told me to divorce his ass long time ago, when I first started to ignore the signs of his cheating!"

Betty stiffly turned her head in Sasha's direction and calmly stated, "You will forgive him, or I just may end up having to tell him about that hickey that you are so desperately are trying to hide under that cheap foundation."

Sasha was floored. She saw the hickey there that morning, and did her damndest with covering it up. Before she was able to respond, her girls came flying out of the house with the items they refused to leave at home. Sasha placed a smile on her face, and gave her girls a hug. She told them to behave, listen, and have fun. As the girls made their way to the truck, Betty and Sasha had a staring showdown. *'Fuck what Betty talking about. I'm going down to the courthouse to file immediately. It's been a few months, too. He probably think I'm not serious, but watch this shit on Monday,'* Sasha thought to herself.

She stood on her porch until she no longer saw Betty's truck. Just as she was turning away, a familiar car pulled up. She wasn't in the mood, but for her to have some type of normalcy, she took a seat on her steps again, until Jade climbed out of her car.

The last time she saw Jade was a little over three weeks ago at Amekia's house. The clothes that Jade was wearing fit loosely on her body, and her eyes were slightly dark underneath. To be frank, Jade looked like she was stressing bad, and Sasha felt horrible that she didn't know what her friend was going through. Jade sat on the steps next to Sasha, and they sat in silence.

Several minutes passed, both wondering who was going to speak first. It shouldn't have been so awkward, but with all of the shit that had been going on, there was nothing but thick tension whenever Sasha would see one of her friends.

"Do you know that right before you pulled up, Betty was telling me that I needed to forgive her whore of a son? She said that in their family, there was no room for divorce," Sasha ranted.

"I know you fucking lying," Jade responded with laughter hidden in her voice. Ms. Betty was a mess, but Jade never knew how much of a mess she was.

"Bitch, if I'm lying, I'm flying. That old bat told me that as married women, a cheating husband is something that we have to adore. If my girls wasn't with her, I would have rock bottomed that hoe something serious."

126

Jade no longer could hold the laughter in as she leaned over and joyously laughed. She'd had a long day of being probed and having tests run on her to make sure the status of her HIV diagnosis wasn't progressing rapidly. She responded, "I'm pretty sure that you would have. You know, she grew up in a different time than we're living in now, and that was how it was back then."

"That was back then. This is now. I told her that same thing. She need to get with the program or stay out of my marriage. Man, these old folks, I tell you. They want to go with how the world is today, but still stuck on how it was in the forties and fifties. I can't take it," Sasha said, shuddering at the thought of taking Betty's advice. She would rather die.

"Don't I know it?" Jade said, and coughed into her forearm. There was silence again.

"It feels like it's been forever since we sat down and just talked. What's been going on with you?" Sasha asked, as she eyed Jade. She was wondering what had her best friend so stressed that she was looking the way she was.

"We won't get on the topic of why, but I get it. I hate that you are the last to know because you were the first one that I met. To be honest, I wanted to tell you first, but the way things were going, and you not answering your phone, made you the last to know. Remember Darion? The nigga that I met, one of the student's parents'?"

Sasha went back a few months in her head, and she remembered Jade telling all of them about this dude. She responded, "Yeah. You pregnant?"

Jade chucked and shook her head. She said, "I wish that was the case, but no, I'm not pregnant. Right before Amekia gave birth to Aziyah, I found out that I'm HIV positive."

Sasha wasn't expecting that to be the news, so the gasp that escaped her lips was one of pure ultra-shock. Never in a million years did she think that someone that she was so close to would catch the deadly disease. Sasha moved closer to Jade, wrapped her arms around her, and shed a few tears.

"I'm so sorry, Jade," Sasha cried.

"It's okay. I've come to terms with it faster than I thought I would. With my meds and things, I should be able to live a long, normal, happy life."

Sasha was astounded at how melancholy Jade was. Not a single tear was in her eye. Sasha asked, "I'm so sorry, Jade. You of all people don't deserve this. Did he intentionally do this, because he can be arrested for attempted murder?"

"No. I don't think that he did it intentionally, Sasha. I just think that he got caught up in the moment and didn't disclose that he had it. I was caught in the moment, and I knew I should have stopped and made him put a condom on. So it really wasn't as much his fault, 'cause I should have known."

"No, ma'am. If he knew he had it and he wanted to fuck you, to reduce the risk of spread, he should have wrapped it up. Have you spoken to him?" Sasha asked.

"I did. And he told me that he had it a while before he met me. His wife was living with it, and never told him, until she was on her death bed. She never took her meds, and lived an unhealthy lifestyle. These things sped up the process for her death. Darion told me that he takes his meds, and get this?"

Sasha raised an eyebrow and said, "What?"

"You remember his girlfriend, Tanya, the one whose ass I had to beat for popping up at my house?"

"Yeah. What about her?"

"She got this shit, too. That's why she was acting the way she was. He told me she was born with it and that the reason why she takes stalking to a whole other level is because she knows how hard it would be to date someone who isn't positive. Just recently, the bitch popped the lock on my screened in porch and smashed in my living room windows."

Sasha was taken aback. She could never imagine going that insane over a man. The fighting shit that she was doing with Amekia was for the birds. She wanted to be cordial with the woman because she was still married to Brandon. Although they were currently not living with each other, she knew there would be a time where she would have to see Aziyah, because she had children by him. Sasha already had it in her mind that she was going to never be friends with Amekia ever again, but being cordial wouldn't hurt.

"Did you call the cops?" Sasha asked, shaking her situation from her thoughts.

"No. I saw her there before she pulled off. She wanted me to know that it was her. If I would have called the cops, it would've just gone unsolved, because I didn't have any proof. I just had to take that L and keep it pushing."

Sasha had no response to what Jade had just said. She couldn't believe how in just under a year, their sacred sisterhood had taken a turn for the worst. Jade's thoughts were saying the same thing, but she didn't want to make Sasha uncomfortable by bringing it up.

"You got some pictures of the baby?" Sasha asked. She didn't want to, but the last time that she saw the baby was when Amekia had the baby.

Jade raised an eyebrow but didn't question it. She said, "Yeah."

Jade pulled her phone out and went to her gallery. She had a shit ton of pictures of Aziyah. She wanted to make sure she captured all of the memories while she could, so when she was on her death bed, she would be able to look back at all of the memories. Jade passed her phone to Sasha. She informed her that the gallery was just pictures of Aziyah. Sasha looked through the pictures. She had to admit that her husband's child looked like he had spit her out himself. Her daughters didn't even look as much like him as Aziyah did. There would be no denying that.

"I never thought that the day would come and I would say that I have a stepchild," Sasha said as she wiped a lone tear from her eye.

Jade felt for Sasha. But what was done, was done, and everybody just had to live through it. Jade turned towards Sasha, rubbed her hand across her knee, and said, "I know this is hard for you, babes, but things happen, and we just got to learn to live through it. This situation is going to get better."

"I don't know, Jade. This shit is just unforgivable, on both of their parts."

"I know."

They got quiet as they both noticed a car pull up. They realized that it was Carmen. When she got out of the car, they realized that Carmen didn't look too happy. She walked up to Sasha and Jade, and couldn't hold the tears that escaped her eyes. They didn't know what was wrong, they just knew that they needed to be there for their girl. When Carmen arrived at Sasha's house, she wasn't expecting for Jade to be there, but she was slightly glad she would only have to repeat what she had to tell them one more time.

"What's going on?" Sasha asked, while rubbing Carmen across the back sympathetically.

"I caught Denise cheating on me," Carmen screeched.

"What?" Jade and Sasha replied in unison.

"That's not the worst part. The worst part is that she was in my house with a man."

At this point Sasha was ready to pass out. There was no way in hell that this shit was happening. She didn't know how all this shit was going down. It seemed like since she'd found out that Amekia and Brandon were fucking with each other, everybody's relationships and lives were going downhill. *'There is too much going on. It's like there is a hex on all of us. Lord, please ease everyone's pain,'* Sasha thought. She looked up at the sky, as she silently continued to pray over her friends. She even went above and beyond, and prayed for Amekia and Aziyah. She asked God to help her heal her heart.

Mimi

Chapter Eleven

"Aww, baby girl, why you crying?" Amekia asked Aziyah. She had just given her a bath and was about to put her down for the night. Amekia had started to put Aziyah down early to train her to sleep through the night. Amekia, herself, was tired, and she looked forward to going to bed.

As Amekia was wrapping Aziyah in her blanket to feed her, she heard her doorbell ringing. Rolling her eyes, she picked up Aziyah and went to answer the door. Amekia wasn't in the mood to see anybody. She didn't want the person at the door to possibly disturb her routine.

Amekia popped the bottle into Aziyah's mouth and went to the door. Nas was standing on the opposite side of the door, and she let him in. She asked, "What you doing here?"

Nas placed a kiss on top of Aziyah's forehead and next was Amekia. He replied, "I wanted to see y'all."

"Well, you know it's her bedtime. You had all day to come see her," Amekia said, mushing her brother in the back of his head.

"I was handling business earlier."

"What business? Sasha?" Amekia asked with sarcasm.

"No. I had to make sure that my businesses were running smoothly. Let me put my niece to sleep," Nas said, while reaching for Aziyah. Amekia passed him the baby and he took over feeding the baby.

"When you gonna stop fucking with her anyway? You was only supposed to mess with her so that you could get out of jail."

Nas didn't want to have this conversation with Amekia for the simple fact that he knew that she wouldn't understand. He did fall deep with Sasha, and he didn't think there was a possibility that he would stop fucking with her. Nas knew that

Amekia wasn't fucking with Sasha at the moment, but she still had love for her.

"Mekia, I don't think that you would like my response for that question."

Amekia eyed him before she said, "You fell in love with her, didn't you? I knew this would happen."

"How you knew it was going to happen if I didn't know it was going to happen?"

Amekia stood up off of the couch, and as much as she wanted to yell, all she had to do was look down at Aziyah and she calmed her down. With her hands on her hips, she said, "Nas, you was only supposed to use her to get out of jail. You wasn't supposed to fall for her. Brandon knows that you are my brother, and all I need is for him to go back and tell her. She gonna think that this shit was a set up. And, I mean, it was, because I didn't want you to spend the rest of your life in jail, especially since I'm the reason you was in there"

"Don't do that, Mekia. You did what you had to do to protect me. I will always be grateful for what you did, but I can't just stop my feelings for Sasha."

Amekia damn sure didn't like that answer. She looked down at Aziyah and noticed she had finished the bottle and was sound asleep. Frustrated, Amekia took Aziyah from Nas and walked her to her room to lay her in the crib. She looked down at her daughter, as she thought about what she had done, and how Nas had taken the fall. It wasn't Nas who walked in on his wife having sex with another man, it was Amekia, and she was the one who shot them. Amekia loved her brother too much to let that shit happen. Nas walked in, and he took the fall for it.

"Amekia, I know how you feel about Sasha, and that feeling isn't going to last long because y'all have been friends for too long. Let me deal with this by myself, and you handle

Brandon. Let him know to keep his mouth shut. I love you, sis, but let me handle this, okay. I love her, but there is no guarantee that she is going to be my wife. I got this." Nas kissed Aziyah on her forehead and Amekia next. He assured her once again that everything was going to be okay. He left soon after.

Placing a blanket on top of Aziyah, she took the baby monitor and went to go fix her a sandwich. Someone's knocking paused her in her steps as she passed by the door. *'Who the fuck is this now? I haven't had this much company since before Aziyah came,'* Amekia thought as she opened the door.

"Aziyah is sleeping," Amekia said when she realized that it was Brandon.

"I know. I just had a long day and needed to see her," Brandon said. His eyes held sorrow, and as much as Amekia wanted to ask him what was wrong, that was no longer her concern. She moved out of the way and let him in. He walked immediately to Aziyah's room, while Amekia closed the door and sat down in the living room, giving him his time with his daughter. Before she knew it, she was knocked out on the couch.

"Amekia," she heard her name being called in her sleep. Slowly her eyelids fluttered open and she saw Brandon standing over her.

"Shit, how long have I been sleep?" she wondered aloud.

"I've only been here for an hour. Come on, let me help you to your room."

"No. I'm okay. I actually wanted to talk to you about something."

"What's up?" Brandon asked as he took a seat on the couch next to Amekia.

"So you know how I introduced Nas to you as my brother?"

"Yes?" Brandon questioned with his eyebrow raised.

"He is my brother, but I don't need you to go back and tell Sasha so."

"Why not?" He looked on confused.

At that moment, Amekia knew that he didn't know that Nas was fucking with Sasha. She was stuck on if she was going to tell him. She simply said, "Well, you know that she was helping him getting out of jail, so I don't want her to think that it was like some set up. That would be just another reason for her to knock on my door, and I don't want nor need that. You saw what happened the last time."

Brandon looked like he was contemplating what she said. Eventually, he simply nodded his head. He said, "I get it. Niggas had enough drama to last a lifetime."

Amekia chuckled and said, "You ain't never lied. Also I want to thank you."

"Thank me for what?"

"For you stepping up and doing what do for Aziyah. I know the situation is fucked up, but you still making it your business to handle it."

"She's my child, Amekia. I knew how I responded wasn't how you expected, but considering the situation, I had a right to. Sasha asked me for a divorce earlier today. I was going to fight it. If I contest it, I wouldn't be in the right, and it would drag out longer than what it is supposed to. I was completely in the wrong, so I'm just going to give it to her, without a fight." He sighed.

Amekia felt bad. Besides all of the shit that transpired, she didn't want to see them divorced. It would affect the girls tremendously.

"We knew what the fuck we were doing, but yet and still did it. Now everything is going to shit, and I can't help but to feel bad. I never wanted it to get this far," Amekia admitted.

"I know, but there is nothing that we can do to change the situation. It's done and over with. I know I've told you before about all of the shit that's been going on, but our marriage wasn't going to last. She was starting to take longer hours at work. I knew she was doing it because I was lying, telling her that I was working late to be with you. To be truthful, I think that was why she was taking those longer hours. I definitely played a huge part with the failing of this marriage, but she did somethings too, to push me away. I think that at the ending, she started having an affair."

Amekia eyes almost dropped out of her head. She would have given herself away, and what she knew. Thank God, he was facing the opposite direction and wasn't looking at her. She asked, "Why do you think that?"

"Her moves weren't lining up. And just like women get a feeling, men do too. She started moving how I was moving, but like her, I didn't have any proof. It just so happened that she got her proof first, and I got caught. My marriage was gonna end up in divorce anyway."

When Brandon had put it that way, she didn't feel so bad about it. She felt like there was nothing that she could have done to prevent their failing marriage. She finally spoke up and said, "I think you should head out. It's time for me to head to bed, I need the rest. I'm going to be going back to work next week, and what little bit of rest I can get, I'm going to take."

"I'm sorry I overstayed my welcome. I didn't know that you had already chose a day care. If you need help with the expense, just let me know," Brandon offered as he got up from the couch.

"Oh, you know I will," Amekia chuckled. Once they got to the door, Amekia opened it for Brandon to leave, but he hesitated. She looked at him confused when he turned in her direction and wrapped his arms around her. He didn't give her time to protest. Even if Amekia wanted to, she wasn't going to. Having his arms wrapped around her felt familiar and comfortable. She hadn't been touched by him since she'd told him she was pregnant, and that was too many months ago, almost a year. She took in his scent, remembering the way he used to make her feel. Brandon pulled his face from the crook of her neck and looked down at her.

"What you smiling for?" he whispered in her ear.

"I wasn't smiling," Amekia stated, as she tried to pull away from Brandon.

"Nah, you was. What was you thinking?"

Amekia was ashamed that she was even thinking such things. She, once again, tried to push away from him, but he pulled her close. She said, "I don't want to tell you because I shouldn't even be thinking the things that I am."

"You can't help but to think about it. I know and understand because I have been trying to keep those thoughts out of my head also."

If her life was a cartoon, then at this moment, Brandon would have heard a huge gulp. She looked at him, the temptation was there, but she knew she couldn't go there.

Brandon made the move for her. He started by kissing the side of her neck and then went up to her face. She was catching chills up and down her spine at the familiar feeling.

"You have no idea how much I have missed you," Brandon whispered.

"I missed you, too. But, Brandon, this isn't right. We shouldn't do this. It's already a fucked up situation, and if we do this, it's only going to make the situation worse," Amekia retorted, trying not to fall for the okey-dokey that she always fell for. She didn't know what it was about him that she always fell for.

"Come on, Amekia. Don't do this to me, to us. You know

that if I wasn't with Sasha, I would have been with you."

Amekia managed to push Brandon away from her and look at him. She said, "And that's the thing. I'm always second choice to the men that I have been dealing with. I have never been first. Granted, when I met Sasha, y'all were engaged to be married, but we didn't start having something between us until y'all were married. Let's be honest, I have always been second choice for you, and I wouldn't even had played myself to ask you to leave her to be with me. What we had, Brandon, is over. I will always have love for you, but I need to be with a man that's going to choose me first."

Brandon couldn't do nothing but respect what she was saying. He shouldn't have even said those words to her. Brandon knew that Amekia was a first-choice type of girl. At the time when he first met Amekia, he thought about leaving Sasha, but Sasha ended up announcing that she was pregnant, and he didn't want to be the asshole.

"You are right, Amekia. As much as I want to fight you on that, I never chose you first, and it would be fucked up of me to do it now. I will always love you, and I'm going to continue to be here for Aziyah. Just because we not going to work on our relationship, doesn't mean I'm going to up and leave that little girl. I'll be happy as long as we will still be friends."

"For sure. We can always remain friends. We got to for that little girl that's up in that room sleeping. I don't want to raise her around nothing with drama," Amekia admitted. She was born into drama. Protecting her daughter was her main goal.

"A'ight, I'ma get out of here. I'll be sure that I'm here a little earlier."

"Please, because she gets fussy when it's time for her to go bed," Amekia chuckled. Brandon joined in with a light chuckle. He gave her another hug, this time not lingering, and left. Amekia couldn't have been more relieved to get the situation between them over with. It was time to move on with her life, and Brandon's chapter needed to be closed in order to do that. Locking up, Amekia turned her lights out and went to bed.

Chapter Twelve

The day at work for Carmen was dragging longer than it should have. It was only two in the afternoon, and she had four more hours to go in order to leave for the day. She was thankful for this time to sit down, while updating charts for patients. She grabbed a bag of chips from the vending machine, and a Pepsi, while she did her work.

Fifteen minutes later, she picked up her phone to scroll through Facebook. She'd avoided it for the past week, since she knew that she was still friends with Denise. Her main purpose to go on Facebook was so that she could delete Denise, but the first thing that she saw when she opened the blue app was a post from Denise. It was a picture. Denise was hugged up with Bilal inside of a club. The knots that formed in her stomach tightened with each second that she stared at the picture. She couldn't believe that she was flaunting this nigga on Facebook.

Carmen didn't think that she would continue to fuck with him. The way Denise had been so distraught the day she came and picked her stuff up, she knew for sure that Denise was remorseful for what she did. Now here she was, flaunting someone else on Facebook, and the nigga that broke them up, at that. Carmen went into the comments and each comment that she looked at was from Denise's family members, ones that she never got the chance to meet because her family didn't believe in same sex relationships. They were commenting heart eyes, congratulating her on their relationship, and even mentioning how cool he was. Anger quickly replaced the hurt that she was feeling.

While they were together, Carmen respected the fact that her family didn't approve, so she only appeared as the friend. Feeling petty, Carmen commented. She said, *'The only reason you're posting fraudulent pictures is because your family won't accept the fact that you love pussy. Stand in your truth, baby girl.'*

With a smile on her face, Carmen hit the send button and closed out the app. She knew that people would start commenting and her notifications would be blowing up, but she didn't care. Denise had done the unforgivable, so in Carmen's mind, telling her people what type of timing they were really on was more than satisfying. The rest of Carmen's day went by smoothly, and when she stepped out of the doors, she had a pep in her step. She needed to see that picture in order to feel better about the situation, and to reassure herself it was okay for her to move on.

When she made it home, she got out of her clothes, and jumped in the shower. Ten minutes later, the sound of her doorbell halted her shower. She was just starting to feel her muscles relax and hated to have to get out. Everything in her body was telling her it was Denise at the door, and if it was, she was prepared to fight. Because in all honesty, what she did was fucked up, but she was in the stage of not giving a fuck.

Carmen was dried and dressed in two minutes flat, racing to the door to open it. Whoever it was had resorted to laying on the bell. Carmen was now irritated and swung the door open. When she did, she was punched in the face. Instantly, her hands flew to her face. She was grabbed by her shirt, and slammed to the floor. When the stars cleared from her head, she saw Denise standing over her, ready to slam her foot into her face. She rolled over just in time. Carmen got up from the floor, feeling blood trickling from her nose.

"Bitch, you got some nerve commenting on my shit with that fuck shit," Denise yelled.

A smirk appeared on Carmen's face. She said, "You can kiss my ass."

Carmen quickly popped her arm out and caught Denise with a jab square in the mouth. She didn't stop there, though. She quickly reached her left arm and jabbed her again. It was Denise's turn to shake the stars from her head. Denise got into a fighting stance and swung her right, but missed, causing Carmen to step in to hit her. The force that was behind the hit would have knocked Denise out, if she wasn't hyped up on adrenaline. She shook it off, and charged Carmen, catching her off guard. Carmen stumbled backward and fell into the living room with Denise on top of her. Denise sat on top of Carmen, raining blows down on her. The only thing that Carmen was able to do was block the blows as best as she could.

Denise was tiring herself out, and her hits weren't coming as fast as she would have liked them to. Carmen took advantage of that and bucked her hips, causing Denise to fly over her head and crash face first into the floor. Carmen quickly got back on her feet, grabbed Denise by her hair, and dragged her across the floor, all the while giving her face shots.

"Get off me, hoe, and let me get up," Denise yelled, as she was trying to get herself up off of the floor.

"Nah, you should have thought about that when you punched me in my shit as soon as I opened my door. You came here for a fight, so that's exactly what the fuck you gonna get," Carmen yelled back.

Denise grabbed Carmen by the ankle and pulled her, causing her to fall to the ground. Both women were tired, but neither wanted to stop. They both were out for blood. Carmen because she was hurt, Denise because her secret was out.

"You done?" Denise asked. Her chest was heaving in and out. She was ready to call it quits. She thought that she was going to come over to beat the breaks off of Carmen, but instead, had her ass handed to her. She got some hits in, but the only damage that she did was the first hit. Carmen wanted to continue to beat her ass to prove a point, but she was now tired, and needed another shower.

"If I get off of you, and you try some punk ass shit, I promise you, you will leave in a body bag," Carmen said.

"I'm not gonna do nothing. Just let me the fuck go!"

Carmen let Denise's hair go, and they both quickly parted from each other. They got up and stared at one another, both women thinking about how crazy they looked. Denise finally said, "You had no right to do what you did."

"And you had all the right to go and fuck with the nigga that broke us up in the first place? I could have maybe understood if you would have gone with another nigga, but the same nigga you was fucking in my house," Carmen retorted.

Denise chuckled and responded, "I blocked you already, but now I gotta answer questions that I didn't want to."

"You always said that you were loud and proud in your skin, but you can't even stand up to your family. You kept me a secret the whole relationship, and I never complained once."

"You don't know my family!"

"Exactly. Even when we agreed to you saying that I was just your friend, I never even met them."

Denise used the back of her hand to wipe the blood that was falling from her forehead into her eye. She shook her head and responded, "You will never understand because I was your first girlfriend. I tried to come out to them before, and you know what they did? They sent me to a catholic boot camp, thinking that I would be saved and it would go away. You don't know the problems that you just caused."

With her hands on her hips, Carmen's face read disinterest. She was done. She did what she felt was best for her to make her feel like she could move on, and she had no remorse.

Shaking her head one more time, Denise made her way to the front door and left. In the past week, she'd thought often of Carmen, and what she could do to get her back. But after the stunt she pulled on Facebook, she was done. There was nothing more that they needed to say to each other, and she vowed to avoid Carmen at all cost.

When Denise left, Carmen closed her house door and cleaned up the little mess they'd caused. She went back into the bathroom to observe the damage that was done to her face. A little bit of ice on her nose would bring down the swelling, but other than that, her face was fine. Carmen climbed into the shower again, staying much longer to make sure her muscles were able to relax. Soon after her shower, she climbed into bed in anticipation of catching up on all of her shows.

***

Meanwhile…

There was one more week left that Sasha would be child free. She had spoken to her girls earlier in the day, and from the excitement in their voices, she knew they were having fun. One of her colleagues at work convinced her to take a week off of work, and as much as she didn't want to, she did. Sasha knew that she needed it more than anything. Her mental state had been out of whack for a few months, and she needed to be at her best.

Recently, she had picked up another high profile case, and they were set to go to court in two weeks. The time off would give her enough time to relax and catch up on the case. The case that she was going to be defending, if she won, would be a guaranteed promotion. With the promotion came more money, and she was going to need it. She decided that after her divorce was finalized, she would move into a new house with just her and the girls, and leave Brandon the house. Sasha didn't want to continue to live in the house that she'd shared with him. A new house was what she needed for her new beginning.

Sasha was sitting at her vanity applying a natural look on her face. She was taking a big risk by inviting Nas over for dinner, but Brandon had been staying at his parents' house, so she figured why not. The girls weren't there, and Brandon wouldn't have a need to come over. Once the plan was set, Sasha hopped in the shower and got dressed in black joggers and a fitted red and white striped shirt. On her feet were black Nike slides, and her hair was done up in a ponytail with a blunt Chinese bang. Her first thought was to cook dinner for him, but when she realized what time it was, she decided to order Italian food from off of Grub Hub.

The doorbell rang just as she was putting the final touches on a nude lipstick. After a few spritz of *Very Sexy Night* from Victoria Secret, she made her way downstairs to grab the food. She was surprised to see Nas standing on the opposite side of the door, holding the bag of food in his left hand, while his right was holding onto a bouquet of flowers.

His cologne intoxicated her as she took him in. He was rocking fitted black jeans with splotches of white on them, a white T-shirt, and a black Adidas dad hat on his head. His chains that he wore the night she saw him at the hotel rested on his neck, and he had a pair of black and white hi-top Vans on his feet.

"You gonna let me in, or you just gonna stare a nigga down all night?" he asked when she took too long inviting him in.

"Oh shit, I'm sorry. You just look fine as fuck," she replied honestly, and moved out of the doorway to let him in.

"Stop playing, shorty. I look fine every day, so this shouldn't be something new to you," he said with a chuckle.

"I don't see you every day, so I need to appreciate it when

I do."

"I appreciate it. Where you want me to put this food at?"

"In the kitchen. You can sit at the dining room table and I'll bring the food out," Sasha suggested. She felt his eyes on her, and when she looked back, they were resting on her ass. She chuckled as she walked over to him and tried to grab the flowers from him.

Nas held them from her grasp as he wrapped his free hand around her waist and pulled her in close. Instantly, her arms wrapped around his waist, and her head rested onto his chest. Unwrapping his arm from her waist, he used his index finger to cuff under her chin and raise her head. He looked at her, studying her facial features, before he lowered his head to place a kiss on her lips.

They were standing in the dining room, so he blindly dropped the flowers onto the table and gripped her waist. In one swift movement, he was pulling her up, causing her to wrap her legs around his waist, all the while, their lips still being planted. His hands roamed freely on her ass, squeezing handfuls of ass. Nas walked over to the table, sat Sasha on top, and pulled his lips from hers. A smile displayed on her lips, while he bit his bottom lip. His dick was rock hard, and wanted nothing more than to be inside of her.

"I ain't gonna lie, I can't wait until your divorce is finalized so I can see you on a daily basis. Shorty, I'm feeling you on a different type of level, and I don't know how much more I can take with having to see you in private," Nas admitted, looking into her eyes.

"I know. I feel the same way, Nas, but just be patient with me just a little while longer."

"Shorty, I'd wait for eternity, if it meant that I could be with you. Don't think that's game 'cause it's the real deal."

"No, I know that you are sincere. I just hate that this is the circumstance. For right now, let's just enjoy each other, and let's eat."

A glint in Nas' eye paused Sasha in her movement as he raise his hand and placed it around her neck, slightly applying pressure. Her eyes rolled to the back of her head once he placed his lips back on hers and tried to take her joggers off. Eating was on his mind, but he wanted to skip the main course and get right down to dessert. Sasha helped Nas pull down her joggers and panties, flinging them to the side once they were off.

He used the hand that was around her neck to push her gently back, so that she was lying flat on top of the table. He parted her legs and looked at her freshly waxed vagina glistening under the dim light. Nas bit his bottom lip as he placed one of the chairs in front of her opened legs.

Nas used his index finger to rub up and down her slit, causing her juices to spill onto his fingers. Nas was amazed at how easy it was for her to get wet with just a simple touch by him. He wasn't even doing anything yet, but there it was, his hand coated in her juices. Sasha let out a low moan when she felt the tip of his finger flicking across the bean of her clit. Her legs were beginning to shake, and she felt like she was about to cum.

"Oh shit, Nas, I'm cumming already," she moaned.

Nas sat between her legs with a smile on his face, as his hand became wetter with her juices. When her legs relaxed, he placed his mouth on her, and used his tongue for what his finger was just doing. He made his tongue do small figure eights on her clit, moving slow, and then faster. Sasha had to have cum at least three more times before he decided that she'd had enough of him devouring her. When he stood up to take his pants off, she was panting uncontrollably.

Sasha tried to sit up on the table, but he pushed her down

again. She couldn't take any more of the pleasurable assault he was giving her with his tongue, so she looked at him confused. She wouldn't dare ask what he was about to do, her mouth was drier than turkey on Thanksgiving. Nas winked at Sasha, assuring her that she was going to be just fine, and he would take it easy on her. In the next few seconds, she felt him entering her, causing her back to arch. Nas spread his legs slightly, so he could balance himself properly before he assaulted her with his dick.

"Nas," she moaned over the sound of her own gushiness.

"Yeah, shorty?" Nas questioned, as he long stroked her. She felt good and tight around his dick, and he wasn't in the mood for talking.

"You forgot to put on a condom," Sasha managed to moan out.

"I didn't forget. I just didn't put one on. I know you on birth control, so you ain't got to worry about getting pregnant."

"Nas, diseases," Sasha screeched, as Nas picked up his pace and pounded into her.

"Shorty, we both clean. I ain't fucking nobody, and I know for damn sure you not. Just hush, and let me give you this dick," Nas grunted. He placed his hands onto the table, and balanced himself on his tip toes to pound her spot. All of Sasha's reservations went out of the window. She knew he was right, so she allowed him to continue what he was doing.

Several minutes later, the table slowly started to move under them, making Nas uncomfortable. With his dick still in her, Nas walked Sasha over to her couch and sat down. When he was comfortable, Sasha planted her feet on either side of him on the couch, and began to bounce.

Nas lifted her shirt just above her titties, to free them from the constraints of her bra. Mushing them together, Nas flicked his tongue across her nipples. Sasha was on the verge of cumming again, when she thought she heard a car door closing. She slowed her pace and tried to listen, but the only noise she heard was her ass cheeks connecting to Nas lap. When she heard her storm door being pulled open, she knew that shit was about to hit the fan. She quickly jumped off Nas' dick and began to look around.

"Shorty, what you doing? I was just about to nut," he expressed, as he watched.

She disappeared into the dining room, and came back wearing his T-shirt, and passing him his boxers and pants. When Nas heard keys at the door, he figured out why Sasha was acting the way that she was. A smirk spread across his face as he slowly put his pants on. Nas made his way into the dining room, where the flowers were. He had hidden his .357 Beretta inside, and that was why he didn't give them to Sasha.

"Brandon, what the hell are you doing here?" Nas heard Sasha ask. She was being loud on purpose. She wanted him to know that it was her husband.

Nas wasn't afraid. The only thing that he could hope for was that her husband didn't mention that he was Amekia's brother. Placing his gun in the back of his pants, he waited against the table in the dining room to reveal himself.

"This is still my house, too, Sasha. I'm tired of staying at my parents' house," Brandon sighed.

"Why didn't you just go to a hotel? Hell, why didn't you just go Amekia's house? I'm sure she would have let you come in with open arms and legs," Sasha retorted, disgust in her voice.

"Sasha, I don't want to go through this with you right now. I just want to get some food and rest."

"Well, nigga, Motel 6 is in the next town over. Go there."

"Sasha, I'm not in the mood for your bitching. I'm going

150

to get something to eat and taking my ass to bed," Brandon stated.

Nas heard the footsteps coming his way. He folded his arms across his bare chest, and waited for Brandon to walk through the doorway. Sasha was following behind Brandon with her heart beating erratically in her chest. When Brandon made it to the dining room, he paused when he saw Nas standing there, against the table that he paid for, with his arms folded. Brandon noticed the flowers on the table and Sasha's clothes on the floor, and looked between the two.

"Brandon, I-" Sasha started, but Brandon cut her off by raising his hand.

"I knew you was fucking around," Brandon chuckled. He wasn't even hurt behind catching Sasha. He found it rather comical, and his chuckle gradually went into full on laughter.

Nas slightly leaned over to look at Sasha with a confused expression. Sasha shrugged her shoulders at Nas, letting him know that she, too, was confused.

"What?" Sasha asked.

"I was just over at Amekia's house, and I told her that I suspected that you were cheating on me. You see, the same way women got intuition, so do men. I saw how you were moving. You damn near mimicked the way I moved, but I just so happen to be dumb enough to get caught. And to be quite honest, if Amekia didn't end up pregnant, you probably still wouldn't have known," Brandon explained, and burst into laughter again.

"You son of a bitch," Sasha yelled. She was angry all over again. For him to throw that in her face was a low blow.

"You didn't think you were going to get caught? Oh man, this is wonderful," Brandon stated as he looked on between the two. He mugged Nas, and whatever Amekia had asked him to do, went out of the window.

"What is so wonderful about it, Brandon? You know what? I don't even care. You were the one who left the house, so therefore, you can leave now," Sasha stated. She was beyond pissed with Brandon. She was fuming at his comment about him sleeping with Amekia.

"Oh, you didn't know?" Brandon asked, still with laughter. He looked between Nas and Sasha. Nas knew it was coming, and he just stood there stone-faced as he waited for Brandon to drop the bomb, so that he could rock his ass to sleep.

"Brandon, I wish you would stop talking in circles. I don't have time for your games right now."

Brandon licked his lips and looked between them, once again. All laughter had stopped as he moved closer to Sasha. She flinched when he got to close, causing Nas to pull his gun and aim it at Brandon. His aim was pointed to the back of the knee, if he was to point it any higher and he had to let it off, there was a risk that the bullet could go through both Brandon and Sasha.

Nas was concentrating on aiming the gun right, when he noticed that Brandon moved away from Sasha, and she was now glaring at him with anger written all over her face. Brandon's whistling irritated Nas, and he wanted to go after him, but he knew by the look on Sasha's face, it would be better if he stayed there. He was going to have to explain a lot, lie a little, and deny any knowledge that he knew of their friendship before he met her as his lawyer.

"You are Amekia's brother? You motherfucker," Sasha yelled, as she full on went into attack mode.

Every blow she delivered rocked his body with surprise. He wasn't expecting for her to hit so hard. Nas tried to block her blows, all the while, trying to calm her down. Then the unthinkable happened.

BOOM!

The gun went off.

Mimi

Friend or Foe 2

Chapter Thirteen

After a long day of work, all Jade wanted to do was relax in a hot bubble bath, with a chilled glass of wine. Although school was out for the summer, all staff was helping pitch in to move things from classrooms. School was opening in a few weeks and there were some minor changes. For the extra money, Jade agreed to help, along with thirty other staff.

When Jade arrived home, she knew her plans were going to have to go on the back burner when she noticed that Darion was sitting on her front stops. She didn't have the energy to deal with him. She didn't understand why he was there in the first place. Rolling her eyes and sending a quick prayer to God to help her deal with Darion, she put her car in park and got out of the car. When Darion noticed that she was getting out of the car, he decided to stand up and greet her.

"What are you doing here, Darion?" Jade asked, as she moved past him, going up the stairs.

"I wanted to come and talk to you, Jade."

"Talk to me about what? I thought I made it very clear the last time I saw you that I didn't want to have anything to do with you," Jade stated aggressively.

"I know. But I can't stop thinking about you."

Jade snorted under her breath and continued on to her door. By not responding, Darion took that as a signal to follow her. Once at the door, Jade paused. She was battling with herself, trying to decide whether or not she wanted to hear him out. She thought that whatever she wanted to know from him, she already got from the last time he was over.

"That sounds like a personal problem, Darion," Jade sighed. She turned around to face him and was met with him right in her face. She had no a space to move. She was pressed against her door.

"You can't tell me that you don't miss me."

"Nigga, I'ma need for you to give me fifty feet 'cause right now, you a little too close for comfort," Jade said, while placing her hand on his chest and trying to move him away.

"Come on, Jade. The last time I felt the inside of you, I performed badly. I just want you to give me another chance to show you that I'm not just two pumps," Darion stated, as he rubbed his hand up her leg, trying to pry her legs open to touch her kitty through her shorts.

"Darion, get your hands off of me. I am not about to be out here playing with you. You have lost your mind if you think you about to put your dick anywhere near me," Jade spoke through gritted teeth, and pushed his hand off of her.

"You think I'm not going to get this pussy? This is my pussy, Jade. I branded it," Darion hissed through his teeth, as he moved his face closer to her neck. At that moment, Jade just knew that he was going to force her into her home and rape her. The revelation of him purposefully giving her HIV shook her heart. She wholeheartedly wanted to believe that that wasn't his motive, but there it was, him admitting it.

Tears welled in her eyes as Jade felt his slimy wet tongue go across her neck. She pleaded, "Darion, please don't do this."

"Nah, bitch. I tried to take the civil approach with you, but look what you made me do. You think I'm gonna give up the best wet pussy I've had in a long time? You got me fucked up, if that's what you thinking."

Jade cried harder when he roughly squeezed her titty through her bra. She could feel his dick pressing against her leg and she couldn't help but to wonder what she'd done for God to punish her in such horrific ways. Darion's hand went around her neck, causing her eyes to fly open, and when they did, her saving grace was walking up her front stairs. When they made eye contact, the tall, muscular man placed his finger over his lips, indicating for Jade to be quiet.

Click. Click.

Instantly, Darion stopped roaming his hand over Jade's body and released his hand from her neck. She was able to wiggle free from in front of Darion, and out of the way.

Her angel said, "Bitch nigga, you was about to rape this woman out in the open?"

"N-n-nah, playa. I was just happy to see that my lady was home. That's my girl," Darion stuttered.

Her angel looked in her direction, and she shook her head, letting him know what Darion was spitting wasn't the truth.

"She your lady, but she crying? That don't make sense to me, homeboy."

Darion cried real tears with his hands in the air. He was begging and pleading for the man not to kill him.

His pleas were falling on deaf ears. The man that saved Jade hated rapists and pedophiles with a passion. He took great joy in ending one of those men's lives, if it meant keeping women and children safe.

Darion said, "Please, man! I wasn't going to hurt her."

Jade walked over to the two men and rocked Darion to sleep. His legs buckled underneath him, as he fell, and his piss slid down his leg. Jade looked at her angel and said, "I suggest you go put that gun away because I'm calling the police, and my lawyer."

"Shorty, you straight knocked him out. Let me put this back in my car, and I'll be right back," he stated.

"You don't have to, the police should be here soon."

"Nah, I'd feel better if I knew that you were safe," he said, and walked over to his car.

Jade watched as he opened the trunk and placed the gun in a compartment. She dialed the 911 operator, and when she was done, he was on his way back over.

"They said that they'll be here in a few minutes. Thank you for your help."

"I don't know what kind of man I would be if I would have kept on driving, knowing I saw what I saw. By the way, my name is Timothy," he said with a smile and his hand outstretched.

"I'm Jade. You don't know how much I thank you. I thought God had given up on me."

"Don't even think that, shorty. Even at your lowest, he is there watching over you."

Jade didn't know this man from a can of paint, and it was refreshing to hear him say those things to her. Her faith in God had been dwindling lately, and with those few short words Timothy spoke, she felt like a fool for questioning God. Sending a mental prayer up to God to ask for His forgiveness, she sat on the steps and waited for the police. She had sent a text to Sasha, letting her know what happened, and that she wanted to press charges against Darion. Sasha texted her back, telling her that she would be there in ten minutes.

During the minutes that it took for the police to get there, Timothy and Jade spoke to each other. Jade was surprised at how well the conversation flowed. It felt like they knew each other for years. When the police arrived, Darion was still knocked out cold, and Sasha was pulling up. Jade noticed that it looked like she was crying, but would ask about it later.

"Who is this?" Sasha asked, looking at Timothy.

"Sasha, this is Timothy. Timothy, this is my best friend and lawyer, Sasha," Jade introduced the two, as she watched the cops drag Darion to the patrol car in handcuffs.

"Nice to meet you. What part does he play in this?" Sasha asked skeptically.

"He was my angel, Sasha. He is willing to give the police

his side of the story, and he didn't want to leave me here, just in case Darion tried to wake up and act crazy."

"Okay, well the police are going to want to take your statement here, and then probably at the police station. Since he didn't actually rape you, you won't need a rape kit done, so I don't think they would want you to come down to the station tonight. Just tell them what happened, and let them know you are pressing charges for attempted rape, and attempted murder."

"Attempted murder?" Timothy asked.

Jade hated that Sasha brought that up at this time, but Jade knew that Sasha wouldn't let it go down. She was vicious when it came to her best friends, and if they ever needed the legal help, she was going to go all out for them.

Eyes lowered to the ground, facing Timothy, Jade said, "I'm HIV positive, and right before you got here, he admitted that he did it purposefully."

Timothy looked at Jade, and then Sasha. With his eyes back on Jade, he placed his hand under her chin and said, "Shorty, when you speaking to me, I'm going to need for you to keep your head held high, you feel me?"

Jade nodded and looked at him in the eyes. Her lip trembled as she said, "I said that he admitted-"

"I heard what you said. Do what Sasha told you, and everything going to be alright," Timothy stated, as he pulled her into a hug.

"I don't know him, but I like him already," Sasha stated, as she caused Timothy and Jade to laugh.

For ten minutes, the police questioned both Jade and Timothy about what happened. They gave Jade a written statement, and went on their way, giving her instructions to come down to the station the next day with Sasha to get the process going for her to press the right charges. Jade's phone had been going off in her pocket the whole time that she was talking to the police, and as it rung now, she wondered who it was that was calling her back to back. As Jade took her phone out, Sasha's phone began to ring, as well, and she stepped off to the side to answer it.

"Amekia? What's going on? Is it an emergency?" Jade asked, as she picked up the phone. She heard a blood curdling scream so loud that she had to move the phone away from her ear. Timothy looked on confused.

"Amekia? What's wrong, babes, I need you to talk to me," Jade yelled.

"Jade! I was only trying to take a shower and now Aziyah is gone!"

"What? Amekia, please tell me you are joking!"

"Why would I joke about that? I put her down for a nap, as always, and went to shower, and when I got out, she was gone. Oh my God! Jade, please help me find my baby!"

"Okay, Amekia, I'm on my way. Call the police now."

Jade and Sasha hung up their phones at the same time. Jade turned to Sasha, and looked at her. Jade said, "Aziyah has been kidnapped."

"Carmen was in a house fire," Sasha spoke at the same time. Both women ran into each other's arms and cried. Timothy looked on, not sure of what to do.

"Sasha, you go to the hospital, and I'm going to go to Amekia's. Keep me updated," Jade said, as she pulled away from Sasha, tears flowing heavily down her face.

"Me and Amekia not talking, but tell her I'm sorry, and that if there is anything I could do, let me know," Sasha yelled over her shoulder, as she ran to her car.

Once Sasha was gone, Jade moved quickly to her car, with Timothy on her heels. When she noticed that he was about to climb into her passenger seat, she stopped. She said, "Timothy, you don't have to."

"I know I don't. But I want to. You want me to drive?" Timothy asked.

He didn't have to ask Jade twice. She threw the key to him as they switched sides. As he drove, she gave him directions, and prayed her hardest to God for him to remove the black clouds that had been placed over all of them.

To Be Continued...
Friend or Foe 3
Coming Soon

Submission Guideline

Submit the first three chapters of your completed manuscript to ldpsubmissions@gmail.com, subject line: Your book's title. The manuscript must be in a .doc file and sent as an attachment. Document should be in Times New Roman, double spaced and in size 12 font. Also, provide your synopsis and full contact information. If sending multiple submissions, they must each be in a separate email.

Have a story but no way to send it electronically? You can still submit to LDP/Ca$h Presents. Send in the first three chapters, written or typed, of your completed manuscript to:

LDP: Submissions Dept
Po Box 944
Stockbridge, Ga 30281

DO NOT send original manuscript. Must be a duplicate.

Provide your synopsis and a cover letter containing your full contact information.

Thanks for considering LDP and Ca$h Presents.

<u>Coming Soon from Lock Down Publications/Ca$h Presents</u>

BOW DOWN TO MY GANGSTA

By **Ca$h**

TORN BETWEEN TWO

By **Coffee**

THE STREETS STAINED MY SOUL **II**

By **Marcellus Allen**

BLOOD OF A BOSS **VI**

SHADOWS OF THE GAME II

By **Askari**

LOYAL TO THE GAME **IV**

By **T.J. & Jelissa**

IF LOVING YOU IS WRONG… **III**

By **Jelissa**

TRUE SAVAGE **VII**

MIDNIGHT CARTEL III

DOPE BOY MAGIC IV

CITY OF KINGZ II

By **Chris Green**

BLAST FOR ME **III**

A SAVAGE DOPEBOY III

CUTTHROAT MAFIA III

By **Ghost**

A HUSTLER'S DECEIT III

KILL ZONE **II**

BAE BELONGS TO ME III

A DOPE BOY'S QUEEN III

By **Aryanna**

COKE KINGS V

KING OF THE TRAP II

By **T.J. Edwards**

GORILLAZ IN THE BAY V

De'Kari

THE STREETS ARE CALLING II

Duquie Wilson

KINGPIN KILLAZ IV

STREET KINGS III

PAID IN BLOOD III

CARTEL KILLAZ IV

DOPE GODS III

Hood Rich

SINS OF A HUSTLA II

ASAD

KINGZ OF THE GAME VI

Playa Ray

SLAUGHTER GANG IV

RUTHLESS HEART IV

By **Willie Slaughter**

THE HEART OF A SAVAGE III

By **Jibril Williams**

FUK SHYT II

By **Blakk Diamond**

THE REALEST KILLAZ III

By Tranay Adams

TRAP GOD III

By Troublesome

YAYO IV

GHOST MOB

Stilloan Robinson

KINGPIN DREAMS III

By Paper Boi Rari

CREAM II

By Yolanda Moore

SON OF A DOPE FIEND III

By Renta

FOREVER GANGSTA II

GLOCKS ON SATIN SHEETS III

By Adrian Dulan

LOYALTY AIN'T PROMISED II

By Keith Williams

THE PRICE YOU PAY FOR LOVE II

By Destiny Skai

CONFESSIONS OF A GANGSTA II

By Nicholas Lock

I'M NOTHING WITHOUT HIS LOVE II

SINS OF A THUG II

By Monet Dragun

LIFE OF A SAVAGE IV

A GANGSTA'S QUR'AN III

MURDA SEASON III

GANGLAND CARTEL II

By **Romell Tukes**

QUIET MONEY III

THUG LIFE II

By **Trai'Quan**

THE STREETS MADE ME III

By **Larry D. Wright**

THE ULTIMATE SACRIFICE VI

IF YOU CROSS ME ONCE II

ANGEL III

By **Anthony Fields**

FRIEND OR FOE III

By **Mimi**

SAVAGE STORMS II

By **Meesha**

BLOOD ON THE MONEY II

By J-Blunt

THE STREETS WILL NEVER CLOSE II

By K'ajji

NIGHTMARES OF A HUSTLA II

By King Dream

Available Now

RESTRAINING ORDER **I & II**
By **CA$H & Coffee**
LOVE KNOWS NO BOUNDARIES **I II & III**
By **Coffee**
RAISED AS A GOON I, II, III & IV
BRED BY THE SLUMS I, II, III
BLAST FOR ME I & II
ROTTEN TO THE CORE I II III
A BRONX TALE I, II, III
DUFFEL BAG CARTEL I II III IV
HEARTLESS GOON I II III IV
A SAVAGE DOPEBOY I II
HEARTLESS GOON I II III
DRUG LORDS I II III
CUTTHROAT MAFIA I II
By **Ghost**
LAY IT DOWN **I & II**
LAST OF A DYING BREED
BLOOD STAINS OF A SHOTTA I & II III
By **Jamaica**
LOYAL TO THE GAME I II III
LIFE OF SIN I, II III
By **TJ & Jelissa**
BLOODY COMMAS I & II
SKI MASK CARTEL I II & III

KING OF NEW YORK I II,III IV V
RISE TO POWER I II III
COKE KINGS I II III IV
BORN HEARTLESS I II III IV
KING OF THE TRAP
By **T.J. Edwards**
IF LOVING HIM IS WRONG…I & II
LOVE ME EVEN WHEN IT HURTS I II III
By **Jelissa**
WHEN THE STREETS CLAP BACK I & II III
THE HEART OF A SAVAGE I II
By **Jibril Williams**
A DISTINGUISHED THUG STOLE MY HEART I II & III
LOVE SHOULDN'T HURT I II III IV
RENEGADE BOYS I II III IV
PAID IN KARMA I II III
SAVAGE STORMS
By **Meesha**
A GANGSTER'S CODE I &, II III
A GANGSTER'S SYN I II III
THE SAVAGE LIFE I II III
CHAINED TO THE STREETS I II III
BLOOD ON THE MONEY
By J-Blunt
PUSH IT TO THE LIMIT
By **Bre' Hayes**
BLOOD OF A BOSS **I, II, III, IV, V**

SHADOWS OF THE GAME

By **Askari**

THE STREETS BLEED MURDER **I, II & III**

THE HEART OF A GANGSTA I II& III

By **Jerry Jackson**

CUM FOR ME I II III IV V VI

An **LDP Erotica Collaboration**

BRIDE OF A HUSTLA **I II & II**

THE FETTI GIRLS **I, II& III**

CORRUPTED BY A GANGSTA I, II III, IV

BLINDED BY HIS LOVE

THE PRICE YOU PAY FOR LOVE

DOPE GIRL MAGIC I II III

By **Destiny Skai**

WHEN A GOOD GIRL GOES BAD

By **Adrienne**

THE COST OF LOYALTY I II III

By Kweli

A GANGSTER'S REVENGE **I II III & IV**

THE BOSS MAN'S DAUGHTERS I II III IV V

A SAVAGE LOVE **I & II**

BAE BELONGS TO ME I II

A HUSTLER'S DECEIT I, II, III

WHAT BAD BITCHES DO I, II, III

SOUL OF A MONSTER I II III

KILL ZONE

A DOPE BOY'S QUEEN I II

By **Aryanna**

A KINGPIN'S AMBITON

A KINGPIN'S AMBITION **II**

I MURDER FOR THE DOUGH

By **Ambitious**

TRUE SAVAGE I II III IV V VI

DOPE BOY MAGIC I, II, III

MIDNIGHT CARTEL I II

CITY OF KINGZ

By **Chris Green**

A DOPEBOY'S PRAYER

By **Eddie "Wolf" Lee**

THE KING CARTEL **I, II & III**

By **Frank Gresham**

THESE NIGGAS AIN'T LOYAL **I, II & III**

By **Nikki Tee**

GANGSTA SHYT **I II &III**

By **CATO**

THE ULTIMATE BETRAYAL

By **Phoenix**

BOSS'N UP **I , II & III**

By **Royal Nicole**

I LOVE YOU TO DEATH

By Destiny J

I RIDE FOR MY HITTA

I STILL RIDE FOR MY HITTA

By **Misty Holt**

LOVE & CHASIN' PAPER

By **Qay Crockett**

TO DIE IN VAIN

SINS OF A HUSTLA

By **ASAD**

BROOKLYN HUSTLAZ

By **Boogsy Morina**

BROOKLYN ON LOCK I & II

By **Sonovia**

GANGSTA CITY

By **Teddy Duke**

A DRUG KING AND HIS DIAMOND I & II III

A DOPEMAN'S RICHES

HER MAN, MINE'S TOO I, II

CASH MONEY HO'S

By Nicole Goosby

TRAPHOUSE KING **I II & III**

KINGPIN KILLAZ I II III

STREET KINGS I II

PAID IN BLOOD **I II**

CARTEL KILLAZ I II III

DOPE GODS I II

By **Hood Rich**

LIPSTICK KILLAH **I, II, III**

CRIME OF PASSION I II & III

FRIEND OR FOE I II

By **Mimi**

STEADY MOBBN' **I, II, III**

THE STREETS STAINED MY SOUL

By **Marcellus Allen**

WHO SHOT YA **I, II, III**

SON OF A DOPE FIEND I II

Renta

GORILLAZ IN THE BAY **I II III IV**

TEARS OF A GANGSTA I II

DE'KARI

TRIGGADALE I II III

Elijah R. Freeman

GOD BLESS THE TRAPPERS I, II, III

THESE SCANDALOUS STREETS I, II, III

FEAR MY GANGSTA I, II, III IV, V

THESE STREETS DON'T LOVE NOBODY I, II

BURY ME A G I, II, III, IV, V

A GANGSTA'S EMPIRE I, II, III, IV

THE DOPEMAN'S BODYGAURD I II

THE REALEST KILLAZ I II

Tranay Adams

THE STREETS ARE CALLING

Duquie Wilson

MARRIED TO A BOSS... I II III

By Destiny Skai & Chris Green

KINGZ OF THE GAME I II III IV V

Playa Ray

SLAUGHTER GANG I II III

RUTHLESS HEART I II III

By Willie Slaughter

FUK SHYT

By Blakk Diamond

DON'T F#CK WITH MY HEART I II

By Linnea

ADDICTED TO THE DRAMA I II III

By Jamila

YAYO I II III

A SHOOTER'S AMBITION I II

By S. Allen

TRAP GOD I II

By Troublesome

FOREVER GANGSTA

GLOCKS ON SATIN SHEETS I II

By Adrian Dulan

TOE TAGZ I II III

By Ah'Million

KINGPIN DREAMS I II

By Paper Boi Rari

CONFESSIONS OF A GANGSTA

By Nicholas Lock

I'M NOTHING WITHOUT HIS LOVE

SINS OF A THUG

By Monet Dragun

CAUGHT UP IN THE LIFE I II III

By Robert Baptiste

NEW TO THE GAME I II III

By **Malik D. Rice**

LIFE OF A SAVAGE I II III

A GANGSTA'S QUR'AN I II

MURDA SEASON I II

GANGLAND CARTEL

By **Romell Tukes**

LOYALTY AIN'T PROMISED

By Keith Williams

QUIET MONEY I II

THUG LIFE

By **Trai'Quan**

THE STREETS MADE ME I II

By **Larry D. Wright**

THE ULTIMATE SACRIFICE I, II, III, IV, V

KHADIFI

IF YOU CROSS ME ONCE

ANGEL I II

By **Anthony Fields**

THE LIFE OF A HOOD STAR

By Ca$h & Rashia Wilson

THE STREETS WILL NEVER CLOSE

By K'ajji

CREAM

By Yolanda Moore

NIGHTMARES OF A HUSTLA

By King Dream

BOOKS BY LDP'S CEO, CA$H

TRUST IN NO MAN

TRUST IN NO MAN 2

TRUST IN NO MAN 3

BONDED BY BLOOD

SHORTY GOT A THUG

THUGS CRY

THUGS CRY 2

THUGS CRY 3

TRUST NO BITCH

TRUST NO BITCH 2

TRUST NO BITCH 3

TIL MY CASKET DROPS

RESTRAINING ORDER

RESTRAINING ORDER 2

IN LOVE WITH A CONVICT

LIFE OF A HOOD STAR

Mimi